Clay's Endless Dreams

GEORGE MILLS

Published in the United States of America

Brilliant Books Literary
137 Forest Park Lane Thomasville
North Carolina 27360 USA

ISBN:
Paperback: 979-8-88945-388-8
Ebook: 979-8-88945-389-5

It gives me great pleasure to introduce you to the third sequel of my writings about Clay finding his one true love. This journey which Clay has found himself on started years earlier after he had gone through a divorce that he did not want, but he had no other choice than to let her go. He started this journey off with "As the Journey Begins," followed by "Looking Forward as the Journey Continues," and then followed by "The Footprint of an American Soldier."

Once again, Clay has decided to share his new adventures with us while still searching for his new soulmate. Now, in case you have not read any of the first three books that I have written concerning Clay's search for his beloved soulmate, Clay is also known as Son.

Contents

Clay was taking his afternoon nap once again. Suddenly, he starts having this dark, deep dream. Now, before he was able to see just how his dream would end, he is awakened by none other than Mrs. Mary, the wife of Mr. John.

Now, Mr. John and Mrs. Mary live in this faraway place, as far as people know. Mr. John owns a motorcycle shop near their home.

Clay had found himself living with them during his search for his new soulmate. They are a nice, middle- aged couple. Clay has agreed to help Mr. John at his shop as payment for them allowing him to stay there.

To this day, Clay has been continuing the search for his new soulmate, whom he referred to as a beautiful wildflower. Throughout this journey, Mrs. Mary has really taken a liking to Clay and holds him in high regard. She's even tried to fix Clay up with her daughter Lana.

Although Clay would never want to offend Mrs. Mary in any way, he is hesitant to start up a relationship with Lana because, in truth, he does not feel in his heart that Lana could be his new soulmate. Although Clay does not completely dismiss the possibility of being with Lana, he wants to avoid hurting Lana or Mrs. Mary. Clay understands exactly how it feels to be heartbroken because of his own failed relationship with his first wife. And so, he is hesitant to start a relationship with anyone at the present time. From here on out, Clay will assume the role of the narrator.

So Long Ago

Before I was awakened by Mrs. Mary while having the dark dream, I remember that I was sitting on a cliff, overlooking an old dirt road that me and my first soulmate once traveled on as young, innocent lovers.

A love unlike any other I had ever known or felt before sat within my heart. Only if she knew how her love caused my tender heart to tremble when our lips touched for the first time.

Today, my heart beats with a great sadness, for when I awoke, my once-beautiful wildflower, who I once held in my arms, was gone, like a great wind passing by on a warm summer morning.

Once, we sat on the back porch listening to the birds sing as we drank our morning coffee.

I once again find myself going room to room, searching for the innocent love of so long ago. I cannot seem to find such a love anymore. All I find are these memories which we had once made years earlier as young lovers. I felt—surely, I knew—deep down within my heart that the heavens had brought us together as young innocent lovers. My tender heart is troubled, and it feels as if I cannot speak as I travel, once again, down this old road with her on my mind.

I look into the rear-view mirror, seeing her face as it appears in a cloud of smoke, as it descends from the old wooden bridge that once connected our world together as the innocent love of so long ago.

Now, I feel as if I have traveled far and beyond in search of a new love unlike the one from back then. As my tender heart slowly trembles within me, my eyes begin to fill with tears, for it all feels like only a dream.

As I continue to walk down this dirt road, the wind begins to blow harder; her face seems to fade like the morning dew on the petals of wildflowers, swaying in the warm summer wind ever so softly.

I find myself now on a new journey traveling alone, searching for my new soulmate, who I know God has placed for me somewhere along this pathway of my life's journey. But it seems like there is no place on earth where such an innocent love exists like the one we had once shared so long ago.

I now find myself asking: has this journey of life been only a dream or a figment of my own imagination? A question which I have found no answer to within myself.

As I find myself traveling down this dark road in life, looking for a place which I cannot find in this evil world, I turn unto the words of my Lord, who knows all things, and these words stand out unto me: "What great love is there than one who is willing to lay down his own life for a friend." Now what greater love can one find than that? Jesus walked the line in my place, for He knew that I could not bear the load of my sins on my own. He took upon His bloody back the old, rugged cross that was meant for a sinner like me. Seeing the blood running down His face, I recall these words as He cried out, "Father, forgive them for they know not what they do and remember their sins no more."

I find myself kneeling at the altar before me with my eyes closed. The eyes of my heart become open for the first time, seeing Jesus's face as the blood ran down like those tears ran down the cheeks of His mother's as she gave birth unto our savior. I knew then what the meaning of innocent, true love really meant.

I am lying here, thinking about what went wrong with the innocent love we once shared so long ago. There are many reasons that is unknown unto me as to why this all took place. It does not seem right to me: the way that our innocent love just faded away like the wind on a warm summer morning.

Now, the warm summer winds have once again come sweeping across the beautiful valley, blowing the petal from its stem leaving the flower bare.

The winds have taken all their beauty away.

Today, I am feeling like those stems who have lost their beautiful petals. I find myself trying with all the strength that is within me to once again find that lost beauty which will make me feel again. One needs such innocent warm love to feel as if they are whole once again.

Oh, my beautiful wildflower from times past, for where can one go to find such a beautiful love like the one we had once shared not so long ago? For now, I can only remember the way you made my heart flutter within me when our lips met for the first time.

Oh man, just when I feel as if I got something good started here, someone comes knocking at my door.

Now I am lying here thinking: should I answer the knock or just hope whoever it is will just go away and let me be?

Oh, wait, that's Mrs. Mary doing the knocking—she has a strange way of knocking on my bedroom door; it goes something like *tap, bang, tap.* I best answer her now that she is calling out my name.

"Clay, are you up?"

Someone Came By

"**O**h, Clay are you awake?"
I answer, "No ma'am. I am just lying here with my eyes open, watching the ceiling fan going around and around."

"Well now, Clay, you might want to stop doing that and get your lazy butt up; there is someone here who would like to see you."

"Well Mrs. Mary, just who might that be?"

"Now, Clay! If you do not get your lazy butt up, I am going to come on in there and put these hands on you like no other had ever done before."

"Well Mrs. Mary, you might just try that. I'll be out as soon as I get my pants on."

"You best be getting a move on, or I will come in there and get you moving."

"Yes, ma'am, I am coming out now."

As I walk into the living room, there stands the most beautiful, sweetest, loveliest lady, whom I have not seen in an exceptionally long time.

I ask her how she's been.

She replies, "I've been doing great, thank you for asking, and how about yourself?"

I answer, "Oh I been in an' out of the hospital. My old heart's been acting up again, and the doctor's put me on this new medication which is supposed to help control the irregular rhythm. For now, it seems to be doing its job, although there are times it still gets out of rhythm. I can only guess it has a lot to do with what I'm doing. Catalina, would you like to take a walk with me down to the ocean?"

"Well, yes. Clay, that is actually why I've come by: to see if you would like to go with me to the beach just to sit and talk."

"Okay Catalina, let's go. We will see you two later, Mrs. Mary, Mr. John."

John speaks up. "Wait just a minute, Clay."

I turn back around, asking John what he wants, and he said, "Here is your pen and notebook."

"Now, John, why would I need them?"

"You might come up with something that you would like to write down for your next not-so-great book."

"Well, Mr. John, just for your smart remark, I will have you know that my very first book has received the badge of London book review's Honoring Excellence. Now put that in your pipe and smoke on that for a while, you old goat."

Mrs. Mary says, "Now you two sound like you are needing a cup of coffee."

"No ma'am," I reply. "It's just that hard-headed old goat of a husband of yours gets under my skin."

Mrs. Mary says, "Yes, Clay, that I know—he does mine as well, but we just got to let it run off our back like water running off the duck's back."

I say, "Yes ma'am, you are right we do at that. Now, Catalina, if we are going for our walk, we need to be on our way."

A Sweet Whisper

As we are walking along the ocean, she leans over and whispers something in my ear. "I am thinking about keeping you all to myself."

"Hmm, you don't say," I reply. "Let's see if we can find a good spot to sit down and rest. Watch the sun as it goes down over the ocean."

"Okay, Clay, that would be nice, but can we just walk a little further down before we do?"

"You know Catalina, I cannot help but to love the peaceful sound of the ocean waves as they come in and go back out. I could sit out here all-night listening to them."

"Yes, it is very peaceful out here tonight. I am going to tell you, Clay, some of our greatest memories are about being out here on this very beach. We spent most of our teenage years growing up on this beach. My family and I would come down here every day after mom and dad got off from work. We would run up and down on the

beach, whenever we weren't playing volleyball or playing in the water."

"Well, sweet lady, as for myself, I never spent any of my free time around the ocean or even around the creek for that matter. All my spare time growing up was spent working."

"Working? Clay, you got to be joking, right?"

"Oh no, ma'am, I would not pull your leg like that. Back when I was growing up, if you wanted anything, you had to work for it. It was nothing like today's teenagers, who think that you should just up and give them everything and they don't gotta anything that would involve work. But you know, Catalina, it's not just teenagers who I see think that way. Nowadays there are also young grown adults who think that way."

"Well now, Clay, I don't necessarily agree with you on your analysis of the situation. I like to think it's their parents who are wanting their children to have more than they did when they were growing up."

I think, *Hmm, now has she been smoking Mr. John's pipe? If so, just what did she have in it?*

I honestly believe a person should work for whatever their needs are in their life and not have someone just up and give it to them. Now, do not take my words in the wrong way here; I do believe we should help one another out when we see them in need, for this is God's word: help those who are in need.

Now with a sweet smile on her face, she turns to me and asks, "Did you see those shooting stars? Oh, Clay, isn't the sky just so beautiful tonight? Do you really need to be going back to Mr. John's tonight?"

Remembering what she had whispered in my ear earlier, I must say that she has not made it easy for me to tell her that I must be going back. I need way more time to think this over before I give her my answer. Now, my first thoughts are if I do take her up on her offer, just where would I be sleeping tonight?

I turn to answer her, and as I do, she is looking at me eye-to-eye and our noses are now touching. I am thinking to myself: *Just how am I going to tell her that I must be going back to Mr. John? I need to help him at his shop tomorrow.*

My mind is telling me to forget about Mr. John and take her up on the offer.

My heart is telling me, *No it is wrong.*

I turn away and look up, saying to myself, *You know, it would be nice to take her up on what she had whispered in my ear.* I then ask myself: *Would it be worth it in the end?*

I turn back to her to tell her my answer, and as I tell her, a frown appeared upon her face. "Okay Clay, I understand. Perhaps some other place or time."

"Catalina, if you like, we can head back."

"No, Clay, not just yet. I would like for us to sit here a little while longer and watch the clouds as they change their shapes, as they move across the night sky.

"Clay, have you ever thought about just what it would feel like to be up there on one of those clouds as it is moving across the sky?"

"No Catalina, I cannot say I have. What about yourself?"

"Yes, Clay, I have, and I believe it would be very nice to ride on one, I would come down here sometime after school and just lay here and daydream about being on one. It would take me anywhere I wanted to go."

"Catalina, you just gave me an idea."

"I did, Clay?"

"Yes, you did. Now, do you recall Mr. John telling me before we left that I needed to bring my pen and notebook with me?"

"Yes Clay, but what does that got to do with me giving you an idea?"

"Well, when you said daydream, I remember this dream that I had once. Would you like to hear about it?"

"Oh yes Clay, I do believe I would. What is it about?"

Endless Dream

"Now, about me telling this story: it's somewhat of a long one."

"Now Clay, just how long can one's dream be?"

"Catalina, it may consume most of our night. Are you sure you want me to tell it to you?"

"Yes, Clay, I'm sure."

"Well, Catalina, it started a few years after I went through my divorce, and I wrote my first book."

"Say what, you have written a book?"

"Yes, Catalina, I've written three books and I am now having an Audiobook done for my first book."

"Now, Clay, that is just impressive. What are your books about?"

"Well, the first one is about a man on a quest looking for his new soulmate after he has gone through a one- sided divorce. At least, he felt it was one-sided."

"Oh, Clay, that is so sad."

"Yes, Catalina, I guess it is in some ways, but he learned that he is better off today than he was when they were married."

"Clay, do you know how long they were married?"

"Somewhere along the line of about twenty-five years."

"Did they have any children together?"

"Yes, they had two. Wait now, how did we go from me telling you about my dream to talking about the book?"

"Well, Clay, I was just curious about your book that you wrote."

"Hmm here I'm thinking you were interested in me telling you about the dream I had one night."

"Yes, Clay, I'm very interested in hearing about your dream, and I'm also interested in getting to know more about you as well."

Hmm, now I am thinking: *She is doing everything that she can to make it harder for me not to take her up on what she had whispered in my ear. Well let me get back to telling her about the dream before I do have a change of heart and take her up on that sweet offer.*

"Catalina, it is about me authoring a story about my time in the military."

"Clay, I didn't know you had served in the armed force. How long did you serve?"

"Sweet lady, I am going to leave that answer for another time, okay. Now, as I was about to say, in this dream, I find myself awaken in this faraway land, looking for a new soulmate, when I came across this desolate place. It seemed somewhat like a desert, where one may have little chance of surviving, and that's when I saw in the far distance what appeared to be this caravan of people coming in my direction. But I'm real thirsty and don't have the strength to cry out, and I didn't even know if they would be passing by my way. So, I used my survivor skills. I find this cactus, and from it, I find little water to quench my thirst."

At this point, Catalina turns and catches me off-guard once again; she asks, "Am I one of those people in the caravan?"

"Now Catalina, you do understand that this is only a dream."

"Yes, Clay, I know it's only your dark dream, but I was hoping that I could maybe brighten it up a little for you."

"Well Catalina, one can only dream right?"

"Yes, Clay, one could say that it is sad that this is only a figment of your own imagination. Now, can I be your main character in this dream?"

"Yes, you can, Catalina. As I was about to say, I found water to quench my dying thirst and I see the caravan moving closer, and then I cry out.

"As they came closer, I heard a voice, which I believe was someone asking, 'Is that person dead?'

"Then, I hear another voice, which was a much sweeter, softer voice, and it sounded distant in a way. I open my eyes and there before me appears the most beautiful face of a goddess, who is kneeling over me."

"Clay, I don't mean to interrupt you again, but is this your dream from years ago, or is it from last night?"

"Catalina it is from…hmm…wait just a minute here before you go asking me any more questions. How about you just let me finish telling you the story and then you can ask all the questions that you may have, okay?"

"Well, Clay, I'm sorry; I was only asking."

"I know that you were only asking, but when someone asks me any questions when I'm telling them a story, it throws me off my concentration.

"Now, as I was saying, this goddess was kneeling over me, and in this sweet soft voice of hers, she whispers in my ear, asking, 'Why you are so far out here in this desolate place?'

"I was still so weak that I could not answer her. She once again whispers, 'I am going to take you with me back to my father's house so that I can nurse you back to good health.'

"Once I was able to regain my strength so that I could speak and move around a little, I thanked her for all she had done for me; and she looked at me with those beautiful baby brown eyes. I found myself once again speechless. It felt as if those eyes had cast a spell upon me." At this point, I turn to Catalina and ask if she would like for me to continue telling her the story.

Oh, What a Big Mistake.

Catalina said, "Clay, did you just ask me something?"

"Yes, ma'am, I did. Have you not been listening to what I've said?"

"Oh yes, Clay, I've heard every word you said."

"Okay, then what was the last thing I said about the dream I had seven years ago?"

While she was thinking for too long about what her answer was going to be, from my mouth flew the words, "Well Catalina, I am waiting."

Now, let me tell you: that was the *wrong* thing to say to a lady like her.

Her beautiful baby-brown eyes were not so beautiful anymore: they became like a big red flaming torch. It was like I had just envisioned the face of the evil one. All at once, Catalina turns away, looks up, and says it is time for us to head back home.

As we are walking back to her house, I lean over and whisper these words in her ear: "Beautiful, you do know

I am so sorry for the way those words came flying out of my mouth earlier."

"Yes Clay, I know that you are, but what you had said has been said and there no way they can be taken back, so we will just let it go at that, okay?"

"Yes, Catalina, I know, but can't you find a place within your heart to forgive me?"

"Perhaps just maybe at another time or place. We just need to wait and see, but for now only time will tell; thank you for seeing me home."

As I walk back to Mr. John's, I'm sure that she is thinking that I am one big jerk. I hear this voice whispering in my ear, *You know, you are so right: you are the biggest jerk alive right now. You may not believe it to be true, and that is the very reason why your first soulmate divorced you.*

"Oh, wait, just hold it right there, you. I did not in any way ask for your opinion, Mr. Little Know-It-All; so just be on your way. I can do my own thinking." It's hard to think straight when you have that annoying little voice whispering in your ear.

Mistake Number Two

Would you like to know something? I have not had a cup of coffee since I started writing about my new adventure.

Oh, wait. I didn't mean to say that part.

What I meant to say is that way before Catalina and I left Mr. John's this afternoon to take a walk down by the ocean, I was hoping that Mrs. Mary has coffee made by the time I get back.

There goes that annoying voice again, whispering in my ear, saying, *You should have taken her up on her offer.*

I reply, "Look, I have told you once before: I will do my own thinking. Now for the last time, I am telling you no means no. Now go away."

Now I am starting to think, *Just what if I had gone and taken her up on her offer? What would it have hurt?*

A much softer voice appeared within me, saying, *My beloved son, you know right from wrong. Now, why have you started second-guessing yourself in this manner?*

"Yes, I do know that it would be wrong, but still, what would it have hurt?"

Now son, will you please listen to me when I tell you that partaking in such an ungodly behavior would have destroyed you both emotionally and physically, and that is something that neither you nor she can ever get back. Once you lose it, it is gone forever.

"Yes, for I know you are right, but is not our God a God of forgiveness? Couldn't we have asked for Him to forgive us both after such an act of disobedience?"

Yes, son, I'm sure you could ask for forgiveness, but just where do you think that would put you in your relationship with Him?

"Hmm. You've asked an exceptionally great question; may I get back with you on your question later?"

Sure, my son. I am not going anywhere any time soon.

Now, after a long walk, I finally get back to Mr. John's. As I make my way through the front door, there's a light coming from the kitchen. I think, *Oh good, they are still up.*

As I make my way toward the kitchen, I hear this knocking, as if someone was at the door. I stop and then turn to look back at the door, thinking surely that no one is knocking on the door at this time of the night.

As I start to go back to see if someone is at the door, I hear it again, but this time it sounds as if it came from down the hall. So, I looked down the hallway, and there I see a dim light coming from under the door of Mr. John's bedroom. I believe explains the knocking sound I hear. I will wait and talk with them tomorrow morning at breakfast.

For now, I am going to bed, right after I've had my midnight cup of coffee. After finishing my cup of coffee, I go to my room and get ready for bed.

Now lying in my bed, I'm unable to fall asleep.

The question that I was asked earlier comes back to my mind. So, I get up and get my bible and start searching for an answer. I come to the book of Numbers and there I find, in chapter five, what may be a satisfactory answer. Now I am starting with verse twenty and will read through to twenty-three. This is how it reads.

But if thou hast gone aside to another instead of thy husband, and if thou be defiled, and some man have lain with thee beside thine husband: Then the priest shall charge the woman with an oath of cursing, and the priest shall say unto the woman, The Lord make thee a curse and an oath among thy people, when the Lord doth make thy thing to rot, and thy belly to swell; And this water that caused the curse shall go into thy bowels, to make thy belly to swell, and thy thing to rot: And the woman shall say, Amen, amen. And the priest shall write these curses in a book, and he shall blot them out with the bitter water.

I am going to stop here with these verses. It is my hope that you will go back and read the entire chapter for yourself.

A Battle from Within

As I am lying here, just thinking about a time that seems so long ago, I hear Mr. John call out, "It is time to get up! Mrs. Mary has your favorite breakfast cooked."

Hmm, I have not smelled any coffee brewing or any bacon cooking.

As I make my way into the kitchen, to my surprise, there is a big plate of bacon along with a pan of tomato gravy sitting on the table. As we sit there eating, Mr. John asks if I would tell them one of my stories about the time I was growing up.

"Well, Mr. John, there is this one story that comes to my mind."

"Well, Clay, what is this story of yours going to be about?"

"Well, Mr. John, it is about an old dear friend of whom I had not seen or heard from in over thirty-five years or so."

Mr. John asks, "What's your friend's name, Clay?"

"Now, Mr. John, if you would just let me tell the story, you would find out. Her name is Ms. Jane, okay? Now, will you please let me tell the rest of the story?"

Mrs. Mary chimes in. "John, will you please stop asking Clay any more questions? Can you not hear that he is trying to tell us about his friend, Ms. Jane?"

"Well thank you, Mrs. Mary, for telling John to stop interrupting me."

"You are very welcome; Clay, you may continue with you story."

"Yes, ma'am. Now, as I was about to say, I was sitting out on my car-porch one afternoon drinking."

"Now Clay, I do not mean to rudely interrupt you once again, but I would bet you both one hundred dollars that I can guess what you were drinking that time of day."

Mrs. Mary and I both just look at Mr. John and shake our heads.

"Now, as I was about to say, Mr. John and Mrs. Mary— " My phone started to ring, interrupting me.

It was my oldest sister, asking me to guess who she just got off the phone with.

I reply to her, "Sis, I've no clue who you were talking too. As you well know, I do not have psychic powers."

She then begins to tell me that she had been talking with Ms. Jane.

I ask her if she had Ms. Jane's phone number, and if so, if she could text it to me so that I could call her.

She tells me that she would right after we finished talking.

As soon as she texts me Ms. Jane's phone number, I call Ms. Jane, and when she said hello, oh my, my heart began to beat faster. It felt as if I had been running a race.

Mr. John asks, "Clay, have you ever been in a race before?"

"Yes, John, matter of fact I have; have you, John?"

Now, as I was about to say before Mr. John so rudely interrupted me. I asked Ms. Jane if she remembered me.

She answers, "Yes, Clay, I remember you."

When she said that she did, I began thinking to myself,

Now just how does she recognize my voice? We haven't spoken to one another in well over thirty-five years or so.

Well, now that part really does not matter, does it?

I went on to ask her how she had been doing all these years.

She replies, "I have been doing very well. Thank you for asking." She went on to say that her and her family was sitting around one day in the backyard, talking. She said it was about the good old days when they were growing up, and my name was brought up by one of her young sister's asking, "Was Clay the one who gave you the pink coat?"

That is when I ask Jane, "How could her sister remember that after all these years have gone by?" I had forgotten all about giving her that coat.

She then says that she had heard that I have become an author. She would like to know where she could get a copy of the book.

I ask her if she was still living in Florida.

She says no; she and all her family had moved back to Petal, Mississippi.

I say, "You're now back in Petal?"

She says, "Yes." She had been living in her grandmother's home for the past thirty-five years.

I say, "Oh, you do not say. I had no idea, Jane, that you and your family had moved back to Mississippi."

She then says, "Clay, I can tell you have not changed all that much."

I ask her, "Where is your grandmother's house in Petal?"

She tells me about where she lives.

I say, "Now, I do believe I know just about where that location is, but just in case I am unable to find it, would you be willing to text your address to me?"

She says, "Sure, Clay, I can text it to you, but you still have not told me where I could get a copy of your book."

I then begin to laugh a little.

She asks, "Why you are laughing?"

I tell her that I have copies of all three books that I have written. I could bring them to her if she texts me her address.

She says, "Oh I will. So, Clay, are you telling me that if I text my home address, you are going to bring me a signed copy of all three books?"

(Wait, there seems to be this ghostwriter who is wanting to try to correct my every sentence.) Now that I have gotten that problem corrected, let me continue with my story.

Now, as I was about to say: Jane and I have been talking about how our lives have changed for us both over the years since we had last seen each other.

I ask her if my sister had said anything to her about me being married.

She said that she did not recall if she did or not.

So, I then tell her that I had gotten married a couple of years after she had moved to Florida and that I also joined my hometown National Guard.

She says that she had also got married to this guy who she met in Florida.

In return, I tell her that I had married this beautiful sweet young lady who my young sister had introduced me to and that we had two children.

She then asks, "Are they now grown?"

I answer, "Yes, Jane, they are, and they are both out on their own. I have only one grandchild who has my heart." I tell her that my wife and I had gotten a divorce after twenty-five years of marriage.

She tells me that she and her husband also have three children, and they too are grown. She only has one grandchild as well. She then tells me that she and her husband also gotten a divorce too.

When she told me that she also was no longer married, I began to think to myself, *Now there just may be a chance for me finding true love once again.* Well, who would know? It only was a thought.

But who can ever know everything there is to know about true love? It can become a dangerous thing in one's life if you let it.

I once felt that I had known what true love really meant, until that one day when I walked in from work, and she said these words to me.

I am no longer in love with you.

"Mr. John, Mrs. Mary, I am sorry about that: I did not mean to veer off course from my story. Now, would you like me to continue with it?"

Mrs. Mary says, "Yes, Clay, please do. You've gotten me curious."

"Now, Mrs. Mary, as I was going to say: Later that week, I found the time to take Jane a copy of my books. We made plans about having dinner one night. It seemed like time itself stood still for me when I laid eyes on her that day.

"Mrs. Mary, I tell you: her beauty was shining as beautifully as a full moon reflecting on the ocean that day. It seemed like time itself had passed us by before we could ever have our dinner date."

Mr. John asks, "Why couldn't you both find the time for your date?"

"Well, Mr. John, I am very sad to say that one afternoon, I was once again sitting on the porch when I received this call saying that Jane had been in this house fire, and she was in critical condition. I only got to see her three times before she left us all for the last time. She went home, as I recall, two or three months later to be with her Heavenly Father.

"My sweet Jane, may you find the rest and peace you so greatly deserve. My beautiful lady, all your heartaches of this life journey you have endured are now behind you. Jane, you may no longer be standing here by our side. But those memories that you leave behind will forevermore illuminate the hearts of your family who you so greatly loved and those who loved you."

All at once, Mrs. Mary says, "Clay, oh Clay, are you alright?"

"Yes, ma'am, I'm fine. Why do you ask?"

"Well, Clay, you looked as if you were in a faraway place."

"No, ma'am, I was only in deep thought. I was remembering some of the great times that I'd spent with Ms. Jane and her family throughout the years when we were growing up."

Mr. John speaks up. "Clay, I am deeply sorry to hear about you losing a friend as great as Jane. I could tell by how you talk about her: deep down in your heart, you cared very much for her. I too know what the battle really feels like when you lose someone you deeply love. When I had lost my first wife, Maureen, it took all the strength within me to keep going."

Mrs. Mary says, "Yes, Clay, that is part of the life we live. I know that if we let it, it will become the hardest journey, but we will endure. As you know, we must unfortunately all face the reality that we will one day leave this corrupt old world behind, leaving loved ones with only the memories we had made together."

I say, "Have either of you seen my pen and notebook? There is something I would like to write down in memory of Jane."

Mr. John replies, "Neither Mrs. Mary nor I have seen those since you took them with you yesterday."

I say, "Well, they just here. Where could I have put them? I know that I brought them in last night now. Did I not?"

Mrs. Mary asks, "Did you leave them with you-know- who?"

"No ma'am, I do not think that I left them with her, now. Although she was the last one to have them down at the beach." I started thinking back to where I had last seen them. I go back to my room, searching for my pen and notebook. I find them lying on my nightstand beside the bed.

So, I walk over to the nightstand, pick them up, and go back to where Mr. John and Mrs. Mary are sitting. I take a seat at the kitchen table.

I start strolling through my memory bank, thinking about the time when I met Ms. Jane. I start writing about those memories of Jane.

Mrs. Mary asks, "Are you sure you are alright?"

I turn to answer her, but before I could say anything, you can probably guess who spoke up first.

"Now, Mary, you of all people in this world should know he is not alright."

Mary says, "Now John, you know that I love you, but you have said enough. I did not ask you anything, did I?"

John says, "Oh no, ma'am, you didn't."

"Okay then. John, keep your watering hole shut from here on out so that Clay can tell me just what is on his mind."

"Yes, ma'am I will just go to the living room and read the newspaper then."

"Now, Clay, will you tell me more about Ms. Jane?"

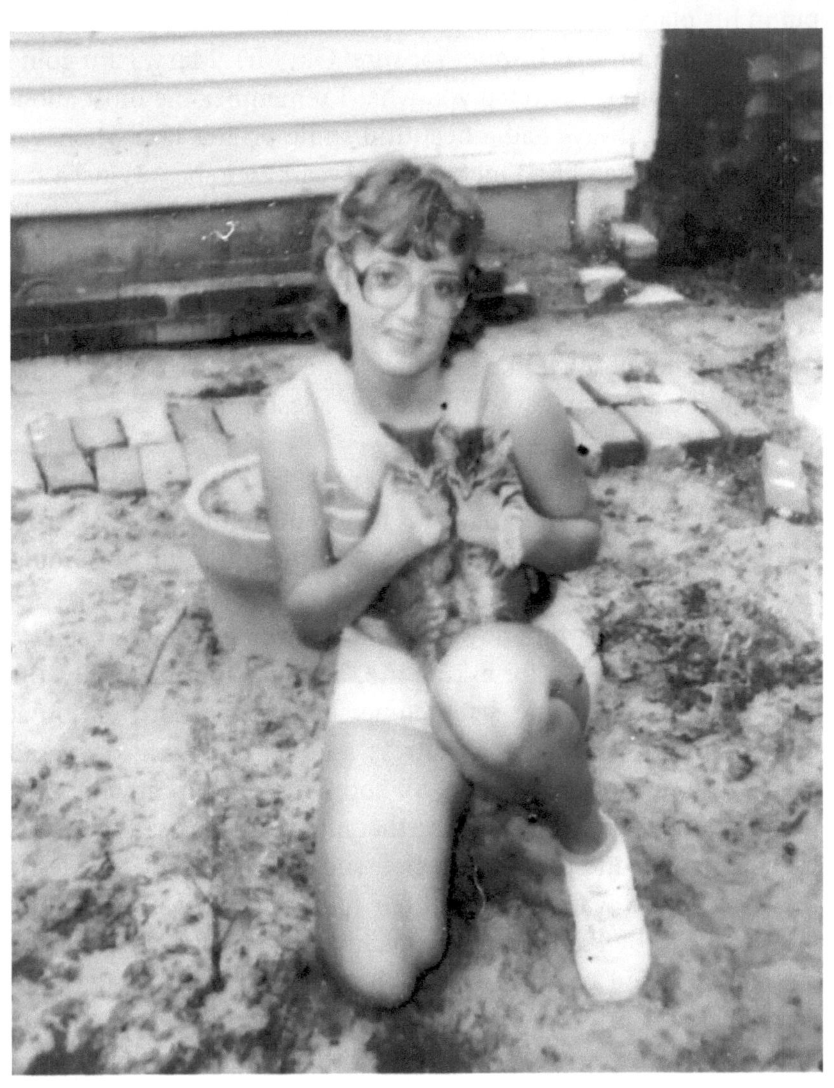

"Now, I am sorry, Mrs. Mary, but until I can stop laughing at the way you told Mr. John to keep his watering hole shut, I'll unable to keep my mind focused; I could start again."

"Oh, Clay I understand. Every now and then, he needs to be put in his place."

"Yes, ma'am that he does for sure. Ok, Mrs. Mary, I am going to try one more time to tell you what I remember the most about Ms. Jane. She always had a beautiful smile on her face whenever you saw her. When I first met her forty years ago, she was just a shy beautiful young lady. If she did not know you very well, she would hardly talk to you at all."

"How long did it take you to get her to talk with you?"

"Well, Mrs. Mary, to be completely honest with you, I really do not recall, but it felt like months."

"Well Clay, may I ask you another question?"

"Yes, ma'am, sure—why not."

"Do you remember how you met Ms. Jane?"

"No, Mrs. Mary, but maybe as I continue telling you this story, it will come back to me. Do you have another question you would like to ask?"

"No, Clay, not right now. You may continue with your story."

"Well, thank you for asking me that question; hopefully, the answer will come to me. I remember her getting her first job at this restaurant, working as a waitress, and her mother also worked there. Well, this one afternoon, for some reasons unknown to me, her mother had to work overtime that night. So, Jane calls and asks if I could come and pick her up after she had gotten off. She didn't see any need to wait there until her mother got off. I said, 'Sure, Jane, I would be happy to come pick you up.' Now, Mrs. Mary, I am feeling like a big man then, for she called me, asking *me* to come pick her up from work. Now, you know me: I am thinking to myself, 'I am going to spend time with a beautiful young lady.'"

"Wait just a minute: how old were you at the time all of this was taking place?"

"Hmm! Now Mrs. Mary, let me answer you in this manner: I was old enough to have my own car at that time. Now, why are you laughing, Mrs. Mary?"

"Because the look you had on your face when I asked you just how old you were back then."

"Well, if you thought that was funny, just wait until I tell you the rest of the story."

"Ok, Clay, please continue with your story. I will try not to interrupt you again, like Mr. John does."

"Oh, Mrs. Mary, you know I do not mind you or Mr. John asking me any questions. It is just the way which Mr. John asks them.

"Now, Jane did not tell me what time I was to pick her up, as I recall. So, I change my clothes and put on nice cologne, and off I go. Well, Mrs. Mary, when I get there, I go inside and ask the host if I could speak with Jane. The hostess said, 'Sure, wait right here. I will get her for you.' The hostess turns and walks into the kitchen for a minute or two, then comes back out and says Jane will be right out in about four minutes. Well, while I am waiting for her, I asked the hostess if I could get a glass of water. As she gets the water for me, out walks Jane.

"Jane asks me, 'Why you are here this early? I am not ready to leave; I still have two more hours.' As she tells me this, my head drops, for I started to feel just like a dummy right then.

"After she had finished telling me this, I say to her, 'I'll just wait for you out in my car.' Now, Mary, those two hours felt like two days, sitting there in my car."

"Now Clay, you could have ordered something to eat while you were waiting for her."

"Mrs. Mary, no offense intended, but you are starting to remind me a little bit of Mr. John."

"Now, Clay, that was very uncalled for; have I not been taking up for you when John says those mean things to you?"

"Yes, ma'am, you have. Now, as I was saying Jane had gotten off from work, and she comes gets in the car with me, and we start heading to her home.

"It felt like I was doing all the talking. She had not said too much during the conversation. It felt as if I was only talking to myself at times. I looked over to see if she had fallen asleep. I said, "Jane, you are not much of a talker, are you?"

"She answers, 'No. How could I say anything when you are doing all the talking for both of us, and you expect me say something?'

"Now, Mrs. Mary, I got a question for you: did you ask me earlier when or how I first met Jane?"

"Yes, I did Clay. It was: 'How did you first meet Jane?'"

"Thank you very much for clarifying that for me. How I first came to meet Ms. Jane. Hmm…now, to the best of my knowledge, I recall it was when her stepdad moved their family into our neighborhood. I had never met any of them until then. I did not know anything about them. Somehow, he knew my mother and her family from way back. Now, it was not until later that I found out how he knew my mother's family. One day, he stops by at the house. He brought his family—Jane's family. Jane was the second oldest child of the family. That is how I got to meet Ms. Jane for the first time, Mrs. Mary. Now that I have searched for that part of the story with you, I am in a great need of a break."

"Yes, so am I, Clay, but you are going to tell me more about Ms. Jane later, right?"

"Yes, ma'am, I promise you I will, right after our short ten-minute break."

"John, have you seen Clay recently?"

"Yes, ma'am, I think he may have said to tell you that he feels like taking a walk down to the coffee shop."

"John, he had promised me that he would tell me more about Ms. Jane."

"Now, Mary, maybe he was thinking that a walk would help clear whatever little mind he doesn't have; after all, you both were talking for a very long time."

"No, John, I do believe that he has walked off down there to see if he could get one of those other girls to go out with him for

Mother's Day. Just so he could say he was not able to go with us to see Lana."

"Wow. Mary, I have known you for an exceedingly long time, and I have never heard you ever use a tone like that before."

"Well John, it makes me mad with him. Now I could understand if he had not known that Lana is looking forward to seeing him. But he does know we are going over to Lana's for Mother's Day, and she wants him to come. John, I am looking for him to find an excuse why he cannot go."

"Mary, you know Mother's Day is two weeks away, right? And you do know that anything can come up, so there no need in getting mad about something you have no control over."

"John you, old sugar bear, for once in your life, you are making some sense."

"Mary that very nice of you to say. Thank you."

"Well, you do sometimes deserve a compliment, John, but don't let it go to that hard head of yours."

"Well, Mary, I am sorry for not showing off my quick- witted intelligence. You know that I'm not the kind of person who would do that, like other people we know do."

"John, did you just say what I think you said?"

"Oh, look, Mary: there is Clay now."

"Hello there, Mr. John and Mrs. Mary; are you both having a disagreement again?"

"Well, just what is it to you if we are having disagreement or not, Clay?"

"Oh, alright then, please excuse me for asking, you old hard-headed goat. Now Mrs. Mary, are you still wanting to hear more of my story?"

"Yes, I do Clay but before you start, I would like to know where you have been all this time."

"Well ma'am, I have been in my room, writing more about Jane, and I drifted off to sleep. Now, are you and John ready to hear what I wrote?"

"Well John told me you said you were walking down to the coffee shop."

"Wait just a minute, Mary, do not go putting words where they do not belong."

"Well John is that not what you said?"

"Now hold on, both of you: I got a question for you, Mr. John."

"Oh yeah, Clay, you got a question for me? Let me hear it."

"Mr. John, when did I ever tell you I was going to take a walk down to the coffee shop today? I know it was not when I walked by you on my way to my room; I did not say one word to you."

"Now Clay, maybe I just thought you said that you were. You both know I cannot hardly hear any more."

"Oh, just how well we know that, John. Now, Clay, will you please continue with your story about Ms. Jane?"

"Yes, Mrs. Mary, first let me refer to my notes that I wrote earlier. After I took her a signed copy of the books, I was calling her each day, or she would call me just to ask how the day had been. She would talk about any events that were coming up at the Church she attended, or she would tell me she had gone shopping with her sisters that day. I am like, 'Hmm, now who is the one doing all the talking?' Now, do not, in any way whatsoever, take what I had just said the wrong way; it's just that I remember what she said about me doing all the talking earlier.

"I will say: Jane loved her church family. Mrs. Mary, why does it feel as if there's a battle going on within me?"

"Clay, one can only find comfort in knowing she's now with her savior, Jesus."

"Yes, ma'am she is, but I did not want to see her leave so soon; she had just come back into my life. Just seeing her beautiful smile could make you feel all warm on the inside and more so when we were talking about Jesus. Now, Mrs. Mary, those words you said about Jesus

brings comfort, knowing we will one day see Jane again, but until that day comes, I will tell you both: I will never forget her beautiful personality, which warmed my heart and everyone else's who had the pleasure of knowing Ms. Jane. Now that's all I am going to say for now about Ms. Jane."

"Clay, from the way you spoke about her, I would say that you really care a lot for her."

"Yes, Mrs. Mary, I indeed did, in lots of ways. If you had only met her once, you too would say that she was as beautiful on the outside as she was on the inside. It is time for an intermission."

"Are you needing a break again?"

"Yes, Mrs. Mary, I feel this tight feeling in my throat that is making it hard to continue talking. The memories of her have got tears coming to my eyes. Mrs. Mary, my only regret is that if I had known seven years earlier that she had moved back home and was once again single, I would try to spend more time with her."

"Now, Clay, that is something that none of us have any control over whatsoever. We have only been giving a limited opportunity here on this earth to search the love of God. We must not take for granted of what little time we do get to have together with our loved ones."

"Yes, Mrs. Mary, I understand what you have said to be true, but that does not fill the void within my heart and in those who loved Ms. Jane. The day which we had to let her go, our hearts had forevermore been changed. Knowing that she could no longer be by our side: now, that hurt. Now, Mr. John, just why do you have tears flowing from your eyes as well?"

"Clay, hearing you talking about Ms. Jane brings back memories: when I had to tell my two young sons their mother was not coming home ever again. To this day, I remember the look on their innocent faces as tears ran down their little cheeks when I told them."

New Time, New Day

At Mr. John's motorcycle shop, time is moving slowly. There hasn't been a single customer all morning.

Mr. John says, "Clay, since there not much going on, how about you tell me about your moonlight walk with Catalina last night."

"Mr. John, it was like the sun going down over the ocean."

"Now Clay, I have never heard an expression like that before. Would you mind explaining yourself?"

"No, Mr. John, I do not mind. It is like saying that it went downhill."

"Now that I do understand, Clay. But what caused it to go downhill?"

"Well, John, as we were walking down to the ocean, she pulls me close and whispers something sweet in my ear."

"What did she whisper, Clay?"

"Now John, I am not going to tell you that, for it is only for me and her to know."

"Well then, Clay, just what caused everything to go south?"

"It was not until after we had found a place to sit down and I started telling her about this dream. Hold on now, Mr. John, before you go asking it was not me telling her about the dream that I had the night before that caused our conversation to go south. I was almost done telling her about the dream when I asked her if she had heard a word that I had said. She answers yes; I then ask her what the last thing that I had was said. Now, while she was thinking, these words came flying out of my mouth: 'I am waiting.'"

"Oh no you did not, Clay. You should have known better than to say that to a beautiful woman."

"Well Mr. John, I may not have known then, but I most definitely know now. You should had seen her beautiful brown eyes: they became like a red flame that could cut a half-inch of steel in half."

"Clay, I would like to hear more about your night with Catalina, but Mrs. Mary has just come in with our lunch."

"Hey guys, how's everything going today?"

"Mary, it has been terribly slow this morning."

"Well, John, I have just broth for you and for Clay, some turnip greens, fried chicken, Mexican cornbread, and, to top it off, my apple pie."

"Mr. John, it's been this slow for the last three months."

"Well, Clay, I do believe it because we are approaching the winter months. As you may or may not know, people seem to slow down the amount of time they are riding their bikes around this time of the year. Now, around three o'clock, I am going to take Mrs. Mary to see this screenplay and I need you to stay back and close the shop for me."

"Just what kind of screenplay are you taking me to see?"

"From what Big Joe, has told me about it, I would say it sounds a lot like something Clay would write about someday."

"Wait just a minute, Mr. John, why do you say it sounds like something that I would write about?"

"Clay, from what he told me, it is about a person who has found themselves be on this quest looking for a long-lost love."

"Now, Mr. John, first thing: I am not looking for a lost love, although I have been looking for a new soulmate. Along the way, I was once asked if I would like to have a screenplay written about my first book. As you well know by me working for you here at your shop, I have little to no income, therefore I am unable to have someone to write it for me."

"Have you even given any thought to writing it yourself?"

"Yes, Mrs. Mary, but I do not know how screenplays are written. I guess I could google how to write a screenplay and go from there; I will just do that tomorrow unless Mr. John needs me to work. Now, Mr. John, if I am going to stay behind and close the shop, then how am I going to get home?"

"Clay, for all I care, you can just walk home and think about the way you spoke to Catalina last night."

"John, that's no way to talk to Clay."

"Mary, you should have heard the things he was telling me before you walked in with our lunch."

"Wait, Mr. John, I did not say one bad thing about Ms. Catalina. All I said was—well, never mind. I will tell you later, Mrs. Mary, when Mr. John is not around."

"Okay Clay, I guess that would be fine with me. Now John what time are we going over to Big Joe's?"

"Mary, we will leave as soon as I can get home and change my work clothes."

"Mr. John, since things are moving slow here why don't you just go ahead and go with Mrs. Mary; I can manage things here."

"Clay let me think this over: now, if I leave this dump boy here all alone for that much time without any supervision, I may not have a motorcycle shop to come tomorrow."

"Now, John, what is your answer to what Clay has suggested?"

"Well now, Mary, since he has now stepped out of the room, I really don't feel I should leave him here for that much time without any supervision."

"Now John, if you feel that way, why did you tell him you needed him to close the shop?"

"Mary, that is only for an hour, and I don't think much could go wrong in an hour."

"Clay, as you were out, John has decided to take you up on your offer."

"That is great, Mrs. Mary; you two go have fun. "Hmm." Now there goes that voice whispering in my ear again: *Now that you are going to be alone for a long time, you can think about what Ms. Catalina had offered you.*

"I told you once, and I will tell you again: just go away."

"Now Clay, just who do you think you are talking to?"

"Mr. John, I was talking to this annoying pest that just keeps whispering in my ear."

"See now Mary, have I not told you something's not right about that boy?"

"Okay John, you told me: so what?"

"Clay, we will see you when we get home tonight."

"Yes Mrs. Mary, I hope you have a fun night out with that old hardheaded goat."

After closing the shop for Mr. John, I head home.

Memories of Mother

After I had walked back from Mr. John's shop that day. I find myself beginning to reflect on the memories of my mother from years ago. It has been twenty years this year since my mom was called home to be with our Lord. I feel like it was only a brief time that we had together here underneath the canopy of heaven.

I do feel within my own heart it was not only about the great times that we once had shared together, but it was also about the sorrow that had been bestowed on us all. The soreness-like pain first found its way into our hearts after we lost dad in a horrifying wreck; then, only a few years later, that sorrow would once again show its ugly face. This time, the pain felt even greater than the first, for you, mom, had been called home as well.

I must say: it took both yours and dad's love working together to help shape us into the adults we are today: the discipline which you gave us. Mother, you were the one who fed us when we could not feed ourselves or bathe ourselves; you would also dry us off and dress us, and if we could not defend for ourselves, you or dad would. Mom, if I could only go back in time and tell you one more time how much I love you and hear you say, "Son, I love you more."

Now as I recall, one memory stands out to me. I had come home from church one Sunday and I began to tell you I had gotten saved, and I gave my heart to Jesus. I recall you saying, "Son, that is great. I only hope you can live up to it."

Mom, if I could only tell you that from that day forward, I have tried my very best to live up to it. I know I have made my share of mistakes over the years; but what I am most grateful for is that you were there to see me though most of them. I know you may not hear me; but I'd just like to say, "I love you mom."

A father's and mother's love for their own children will forever outshine all the other love we think we may have found in another person. There may come a time in your life journey when your soulmate might tell you that he or she has had enough of loving you and just walks away. It leaves you wondering if their love was as true of a love as the day you both first met.

I see a flash of light come through the living room window. It's Mr. John and Mrs. Mary.

As Mrs. Mary comes through the front door and sees me sitting in Mr. John's chair, she asks me, "Why are you still up this late at night?"

"Mrs. Mary, I did not realize it was 2:00 a.m. I have been sitting here thinking about my mother; you know Mother's Day is only two weeks away?"

"Yes, Clay, John and I had made plans to go to my daughter Lana's for half a day and then go on over to his son's house; do you have any plans, know how you're going to spend your day?"

"No ma'am, I have not made any at the moment."

"Well Clay, you know that you are more than welcome to go with us; and you also know that Lana would love to see you. Whenever she calls, she is always asking about you."

Now I am like, "Hmm," thinking to myself, *You do not say? I do know Lana is single and very pleasant to look upon.*

"Yes, Clay, Mary and I both would like for you to join us."

"Mr. John and Mrs. Mary, that's very thoughtful of you both to ask me, but may I do some thinking before I give you my answer?"

"Yes Clay, but I will need to know by next Wednesday, for Lana and I need to know how much food to cook."

"Yes Mrs. Mary, I will let you know by Wednesday.

Now, good night—or in this case, good morning."

"Yes Clay, we will see you at daybreak: you have a lot of unfinished storytelling to do."

I do? Just what stories would that be? I think to myself.

As I lie in bed, a question from within starts to weigh heavy on my mind. I am unable to sleep, and once again, I turn to my bible, hoping that I can find an answer to this question from within myself. I turn to the book of Romans, and I start in chapter two, verse nineteen, and read though verse twenty-four. I am reading the "King James."

(19) And art confident that thou thyself art a guide of the blind, a light of them which are in darkness, (20) An instructor of the foolish, a teacher of babes, which hast the form of knowledge and of the truth in the law. (21) Thou therefore which teaches another, teaches thou thyself? Thou that preaches a man should not steal, dost thou steal? (22) Thou that sayest a man should not commit adultery, dost thou commit adultery? Are thou that abhorrers' idols, dost commit sacrilege? (23) Thou that markets thy boast of the law, through breaking the law dishonors' thou God. (24) For the name of God is blasphemed among the Gentiles through you, as it is written.

Early Dawn

Before the sun could break through the window, I hear Mr. John calling me. "Hey, Clay, it's time to rise! I got the coffee going and Mrs. Mary's asking how you would like your eggs cooked this morning."

I am like, *Can I not get any sleep at all around this place?*

I get up and stumble my way to the bathroom only to find there is no ----------. If you wish, you may fill in the blank yourself. I need to take a shower to refresh myself, as one might say.

While I am taking my shower, I recall what Mr. John had said about me not being right in the head. I may have just produced an effective way to show him just how off I am. I sing at the top of my voice.

Let me tell you about the time when I was born.

It was my mom and the doctor and a few nurses in the delivery room. The doctor says, "Ma'am, I do not have great news to tell you. For the life of me, I cannot send this boy back. He just does not seem to be all right, for reasons unknown to me, although he does have everything intact for a child of his size. I also must tell you that he will have some kind of problems throughout his life if he lives to see adulthood."

After telling her that, he turns me over and begins spanking my behind. I will say that the doctor was not wrong: from that day forward, I have seen my share of problems and it all started by him spanking my behind.

If only I could have seen the look on Mr. John's face as I was trying to sing my birthday song.

After I get dressed, I make my way to the kitchen only to find Mrs. Mary there alone. I ask her, "Where's Mr. John?"

"Clay, he heard you trying to sing in the shower. He got up, shaking his head, and walked out on to the back porch, saying, 'Lord, if there any way possible, please, please for the life of me, help that boy; I do not know just how much more I can take.'"

"Mrs. Mary, may I ask you a question?"

"Sure you can, Clay."

"Thank you, Mrs. Mary. May I just refer to you as just Mary from here on out?"

"Yes, Clay, you surely may refer to me as just Mary. Now, would you step out the door and tell that hard- head John it's time to eat."

"Yes, ma'am I sure will. Hey, you hardheaded old goat, Mary said it's time for you to come in and eat before your food get any cooler."

"Now Clay, who are you calling a hardheaded old goat, when you are the one who's not all there in the head?"

"Now Mr. John ever since I have been acquainted with you, you have told me that I am not right in the head; I would like to know why you would say that."

"You have the audacity to stand there and ask me that after the way you were carrying on earlier in the shower?"

"John, I was only joking around. Now come on in and let's eat; I am hungry."

"Clay, you are always hungry. If you ate a whole cow, you would still be hungry."

"Wait now, John, you know that is not all true. I just do not eat a lot at one time."

"Clay, have you giving any more thought to your plans for Mother's Day?"

"Yes, ma'am. As it stands for now, I going to the cemetery, and afterward, if it is ok with you, Mrs. Mary, I will then join you both at Lana's."

"Clay, we understand you wanting to go visit your mother's grave."

"Yes Mrs. Mary, I been missing mom a lot here lately; there a lot of things that have gone on in my life over the past few years that I wish I could talk with her about. Oh, if only I could hear her sweet voice once again."

"Clay, I want you to finish telling us about your night out with Catalina."

"John, don't be so rude."

"Mary, it was not my intention to be rude to the dummy. I just did not want him to get all emotional again."

"Now, John, if you insist on hearing about my night out with Catalina, I am going to insist that you hold all your smart comments until I am done talking."

"Yes, Clay, I will wait until you have finished."

"Hmm. Catalina and I were sitting on the beach, and I was telling her about the dream I had about you and Mrs. Mary."

"Oh, you just hold it right there, mister; you been having dreams about me and Mary?"

"John, one more outburst like that, and I will no longer be telling any of my stories to you. Now, I was telling her that in this dream, you and Mrs. Mary were helping me to write about the time I had spent in the military. But before we could finish drafting it, for reasons unknown to me, I told both of you I was going to get on my motorcycle and ride off into the sunset, leaving the rest of my story untold.

"That's when I think I heard Mrs. Mary telling you, John, that there is someone knocking at front door. Now, John, that was when I awoke from this dream; Mrs. Mary was knocking on my bedroom door, saying, 'Clay, oh, Clay, there is someone here who would like to see you.'"

"Now Mary did you understand any of that mumbo jumbo he just told us?"

"Well yes, I did, John."

"Now John, it is your turn to tell me about this screenplay you and Mary saw last night."

"Clay, even if I told you about it, I believe that you would not understand, because you don't have the knowledge to know anything about screenplays."

"Hmm." I guess he just told me that I was ignorant. Is what your takeaway as well? At one point or another in my story here, I am going to show him that I am not as dumb as he may think I am.

"Clay."

"Yes, Mrs. Mary?"

"Do not listen to John. He was telling me, on our way back home last night, that he did not fully understand the screenplay that well."

"Yes, Mary, I did tell you that, because it did not make any sense. I know when something makes sense, unlike Clay here. Mary, you heard me telling Big Joe that if he could get Floyd, who is one of his screenwriters, to fill in the missing storylines in the right places, it could have the potential of making a good movie. Big Joe said that he would talk with Floyd and see if he could figure out a way to bring the story together."

"Now John, you got my curiosity going once again."

"How could I get someone like yourself curious?!"

"Well, John, you got—oh, wait now, you didn't just say to me what I am thinking you said?"

"Yes, he did Clay, for I heard him say it also."

"Thanks, Mrs. Mary, for confirming that he did say it.

Now John, with the way you've been throwing those smart remarks at me, I am going to my room, getting on my computer, and googling how to write a screenplay."

"Yes, why don't you do that Clay? I will turn the computer on for you since you don't have the brains to know how to. You don't even know how to search anything on google."

"Naw, John, I believe that I can putty much handle this on my own."

"Clay, you cannot even pronounce 'pretty' right, and you think you going to be able to google how to write a screenplay? I don't think so."

"Now John, you once again go way too far with your smart remarks to Clay."

"Well, Mary, I cannot help myself. You know I only calling things as I know them to be true."

"Mrs. Mary, it is all good, I am going to get my computer, pen, and notebook, and then I'm walking down to the beach for a little while. Now, if you need me for anything, that is where I will be."

"Okay, Clay, thanks you for letting me know where you are going to be."

As I am walking down to the beach to research how to write a screenplay, I meet Ms. Gloria, and we say hello to each other and start talking.

I ask her if she would like to join me for a walk alone the beach.

She replies, "Yes, I would love to, Clay. I see you have your computer along with your pen and notebook: are you going to do some writing while we are at the beach?"

"Yes, Gloria, I am going to try and see if I can somehow maybe write a small screenplay for Mr. John."

"Clay, why would you write a screenplay for Mr. John?"

"Well Gloria, for the past three months or so, it seems to me that Mr. John has, for reasons unknown to me, been saying things to me like, 'Clay, you must be one of the most uneducated persons that I have ever met in all my life.' Now Gloria, can I ask you a question?"

"Clay, I have no problem with you asking me a question."

"Gloria, do you know anything about how a screenplay is written?"

"Oh no Clay, I never took drama class back in school, for I never was interested in acting."

"Gloria, I must say: you do have a beautiful figure and you also have the personality to be one, if you so choose. Now Gloria, why are blushing? Was it something I said?"

"Thank you for those kind words. No one has ever said them to me before. Gloria, would you like to help me out here? I need to produce a delightful story line to start the screenplay off with."

"Well Clay, let me think about this for a minute; ok, what if you start it off with something that you know about? Let us say, for instance, it could be about two people who meet for the first time on the beach, and they become good friends."

"Now Gloria, that's an excellent idea. I'm glad you decided to come along with me; you have been an immense help. When I get back to Mr. John's this afternoon, I will start working on this idea you have giving me. I will show that old goat that I am not as unintelligent as he thinks I am. Now, Gloria, would you like for me to see you home?"

"No, Clay, I am going to visit one of my girlfriends' once we leave here, but thanks for asking."

"Gloria, I hope we can get together again and spend more time down here at the beach one day soon."

"Oh yes Clay, I would like that. What do you think about us meeting this coming Monday afternoon after I get off from work; say, we could meet down at the coffee shop? Then afterward we could take our walk down here for a moonlight stroll."

"Okay, sounds good to me. Bye for now."

After leaving Gloria at the beach, I begin my long walk back to Mr. John's. As I walk, I begin to wonder where this scene might just take place, and just what names I could use for the characters, and who would be acting the part. This within itself is going to be quite an adventure, unlike any other I have every undergone before. Stay with me until the end of this adventure.

"Clay, are you in your room talking to yourself?"

"No, Mrs. Mary, I just walked in from being at the beach with Gloria."

"Oh, ok. How is Ms. Gloria?"

"Well, Mrs. Mary, I guess you could say she's doing great. She got to spend time alone with me at the beach today."

"Really now, Clay?"

"Yes, Mrs. Mary, she really did. Now, I am going to my bedroom to start working on my new adventure."

"Clay, may I ask: just what is this new adventure that you have come up with?"

"Mrs. Mary, do you recall us talking earlier about me possibly writing a screenplay? Well, that is what I'm about to go do, so if you need me, I'll be in my room."

"Okay Clay, but before you go, may I ask what your screenplay is going to be about?"

"Mary, you are going to have to wait until I am done with it."

My Version of a Screenplay

SCENE ONE TAKE ONE

It is high noon on a sizzling summer day in June, and the temperature once again has reached an all-time high in Susanna's hometown of Biloxi, Mississippi.

Susanna is walking on the beach all alone, wearing this hot two-piece pink bikini with only a blue beach- towel around her slender-sexy waist. She sees Daniel also walking alone carrying his surfboard.

Her face begins to light up as he gets closer. She starts to wave her hand for him to come over. As he gets to where she is, she takes her beach-towel from around her waist and lays it on the hot-sand. They say hello to each other.

Daniel says, "Susanna, I got to say: you are looking very lovely today in that hot pink bikini."

"Well thank you, Daniel, that was genuinely nice of you to say. May I ask how you've been doing over the past two weeks?"

"Now Susanna, I have been doing very well, thank you; although I must say that these feverish temperatures we are having has start too affect me. What are your thoughts, Susanna, on these unusual feverish temperatures we been having for the past two weeks?"

"Daniel, I do not know what to think, to be honest, but I will say: if it keeps getting any hotter this month, I believe I will become a mermaid and just live in the ocean until winter comes."

"Hmm, now, Susanna, I would love to see you do that, for you and me both know that is not possible—unless you have magical powers, which I do not believe you own."

"No, Daniel, I do not have any magical power; that was only a figure of speech. I am not one of your everyday run-of-the-mill blondes, as you well know."

"Well now! Excuse me. Susanna, would you like to take my surfboard out and see if you can catch a wave to ride?"

"Daniel, to be honest with you, I have not been out on a surfboard for and exceedingly long time. Are you sure you do not mind me taking it out?

"Hmm, let me think this over for just a second or two. Well, Susanna, after thinking it over, I will go out with you and we can just sit out there together and talk for a little while; what do you say about that, Susanna?"

"Daniel, I am fine with us sitting out there and talking; but just what are we going to do if there are waves that start to come in?"

"Now Susanna, we are not going that far out, I promise you."

"Well Daniel, I am ready to get wet; the longer we sit here, the hotter it seems to get by the minute."

Now Daniel starts thinking to himself, as he is slightly shaking his head, *Oh you believe me, Susanna: you are looking ridiculously hot alright, sitting there in that two- piece bikini.* "Now, Susanna, before we get in the water, would you like for me to rub sunscreen on your shoulders and back?"

"Well, yes, Daniel, please. And if you do not mind, could you also please rub sunscreen on the back of my legs?"

"No, Susanna, I do not mind at all, but you need to lay on your stomach if I am going be putting some on the back of your legs."

"Sure Daniel, I will lay on my stomach, so long as you do not take that long putting on the sunscreen."

Now, I first start rubbing sunscreen on Susanna's shoulders, then I start slowly moving my way down onto her smooth, soft, unblemished back, and then work my way downward onto her delightful, sexy, long legs. I start thinking, *Oh man this could become a major workout.*

"Now, Daniel, what is taking you so long?"

Before I could even begin to answer her, I start to wonder that maybe she would like for me to rub sunscreen on her lovely stomach as well.

"Now, Susanna, will you just give me one more minute here, and I will be finished. I only need to put some more on your left leg to make sure you're fully protected from the sun."

"Well, Daniel, can you please hurry, I would like to get in the water before it gets any hotter."

While they are sitting out on Daniel's surfboard talking, in comes this big, humongous wave which neither she nor Daniel had seen coming.

It knocks them both off the surfboard, and Susanna hits her head, becoming disoriented.

Daniel has no clue what just happened; after coming up from under the water, he begins asking Susanna where she is.

As he looks around to find her, he sees her swimming away from the shoreline.

He takes out after her as fast as he can, hoping he can catch her.

After he caught up with her, Daniel says, "Susanna, where do you think you are going?"

Susanna answers, "I do not know who you are calling Susanna, but as for me, I am heading back toward the shoreline."

"No, the shoreline is behind us. Susanna, why are you looking at me with that disturbed look on your face?"

"Susanna? I have told you that I do not know this person. Are you sure the shoreline is back behind us?"

"Yes, Susanna, I am sure that the shoreline is back behind us. Now will you please come back with me?"

"Well, I guess so, if you are sure the shoreline is back behind us."

"Yes, Susanna, I am insisting we turn back and head the other way. I have this feeling there is something seriously wrong with you."

"Why do you feel there is something wrong with me?"

"Well Susanna, the first thing is that you do not recognize your own name, and you were heading away from the shoreline. I think you need to be checked out by a doctor."

As Daniel gets closer to the shore with Susanna, he starts carrying her and begins calling out for help. There are only a few people on the beach at this time who hear him calling out for help, and they start running to their aid.

One of them asks Daniel, "What is wrong with her?"

Daniel says, "I do not know; can someone here please go call for the paramedics?"

"The End of Scene One."

Now, after I had gone back and worked out all the incorrect pronunciations and punctuation errors, I feel as if I am now ready to start my second scene of the screenplay.

Are you ready to see just how this screenplay is going to end? I know I am, but like I had said in the beginning of the story, this will be quite an adventure, and so far, it has not in disappointed me.

"Scene Two Take Two"

The paramedics are now on the scene. The first paramedics to reach Susanna ask her to say her name.

Susanna still doesn't know what had just happened. She begins to look around her to see if she could recognize someone. She then turns back to the paramedics and says, "I am unsure just where I am at, but it looks like I am on a beach."

Then the paramedics ask, "Well, can you tell me what happened to you?

Susanna, still not sure of herself, begins to shake her head left and right.

The paramedics turn to Daniel and ask him if he knows her, and if so, could he tell them what had happened to her.

Daniel begins telling them what had happened.

After Daniel had told the paramedics what had taken place, the paramedics look back at Susanna and say, "Young lady, we are going to take you for a ride in the ambulance to the hospital."

Susanna looks at the paramedics and says, "Now, why are you going to give me a ride to the hospital?"

The paramedics answer, "I do believe you have a bad concussion, but we will let the doctor decide that once we get you to hospital. He may ask for a CT-Scan, just to be sure you do not have any bleeding in your brain."

As the paramedics are putting Susanna in the ambulance to take her to the hospital, Daniel asks one of the paramedics if he could ride with her.

The paramedics asked him if he was related to her. Daniel answers, "No, I am not related to her."

The paramedics answer, "Daniel, then you cannot.

Only a member family can ride with the patient."

Daniel then asks, "Well, can you at least tell me the name of hospital you are taking her to?"

"We are taking her to Westmore hospital. It is just off interstate 201, right before you get to Westmore road 203. There is no way you can miss it if you stay on road 202."

Some time has gone by before Daniel could go check on Susanna. He has to go home and take a shower and change his clothes.

After Daniel finally gets to the hospital, to check on Susanna, he finds out that she has been sent over to another hospital. The nurse tells him that she was transferred so she could receive further treatment for her head injury.

Daniel asks, "Well, what hospital did they sent her to for better treatment?"

The nurse said the doctor felt she needed to be transfer up to Morehead hospital.

Daniel says, "Morehead? Where is that? I have never heard of it."

The nurse says, with a beautiful smile on her face, "Sir it is about twenty-five miles up the interstate. Get back on the interstate, go two miles, and take exit B-91 onto South state street 409. Stay on it for five miles, then turn right onto North state street for two or three miles; you will see the hospital on your left."

Daniel runs back to his truck and off he goes, but just before he gets out of the parking lot, he stops.

The film director calls, "Cut!" and he asks Daniel as to why he had stopped in the middle of a scene.

Daniel answers, "I have forgotten the way which that hot gorgeous nurse said I should go. Now I am going to google how to get to Morehead hospital."

The film director looks at Daniel with this disgusted look on his face and says, "Now Daniel, if you were not Big Joe's pick for the leading actor for this movie, I would fire you right here and now. Why did you not think of doing that as she was giving you the directions in the first place?"

Daniel looks over at the film director and says, "I got it now; I am ready."

The director shakes his head and says, "Scene two, take three. Places, everyone! And…action."

Daniel shifts the gear into drive and lays on on the accelerator, pushing it to the floorboard and leaving rubber for twenty feet as he leaves the parking lot.

The film director just shakes his head in disbelief.

About a mile or so later, Daniel gets blue-lighted by this highway patrol officer. The officer pulls him over onto the side of the road. Daniel is looking in his driver's- side mirror as the officer is getting out of the patrol cruiser. He watches the officer as she approaches his truck.

Now, as she is walking alongside the truck, he starts thinking to himself, *Hmm. Now that is one gorgeous officer right there; her uniform sure fits her in all the right places.*

The officer walks very slowly up to the window, and she puts her left hand on the door.

Daniel says, "Good afternoon, officer, I hope you do not mind me saying this, but you are the finest-looking officer I've had the pleasure of being pulled over by in all my life."

Now the officer, being an actor herself, just plays right along with Daniel. "So, sir, what you are telling me here is that you think I am a fine-looking woman. I am not all that into betting what you might say, but I am willing to bet that you were also thinking that I like to just dress up in these skintight patrol officer's uniforms and pull over jerks like yourself. Now, sir, would you like to just step out of your truck now, and let us see if my nice new shiny handcuffs might fit you?"

Daniel started thinking to himself once again, *Now she could be one those wild ones.* He replies, "Oh no ma'am, I cannot today, for you see, I am working."

The officer asks him, "Well, sir, just what kind of work do you do?"

Daniel says, "Ma'am, I work for the movie director who is sitting right over there with his crew; they have been filming everything that we had said."

The officer says, "So that explains why you were going over a hundred."

"Yes, ma'am, I am on my way to the hospital to check on Susanna."

The officer asks Daniel if he would like for her to escort him to the hospital.

Daniel says, "Sure, why not? That is, if you do not mind helping me out."

She turns and then walks a few steps back towards her cruiser, stops, turns, and walks back to Daniel and asks, "Just what is the name of the hospital are you going to?"

Daniel says, "Now, ma'am, the nurse told me back at Westmore that the name of the hospital is Morehead. I do hope you know where it is located?"

Mike, who is the film director, is sitting with his crew, waiting with great suspense, wondering what is to come next.

While they are waiting to see just what Daniel's next move is going to be for this one scene, back at the studio, Big Joe, who is the producer of this film starts walking up and down the hallway, wondering why they are not back. Big Joe walks back into his office and asks his sectary if she could get Mike on the radio for him. Once Big Joe's secretary gets Mike on the radio, she then hands it over to him.

Big Joe asks Mike why they are not back at the studio already. "Mike, I am sure you know we are on a very tight schedule, not to mention a small budget too."

Now Mike is unaware that he is being pranked by Big Joe and all the rest of the crew. Mike answers, "Sir, your leading actor for this movie, Daniel, is wanting to do his own thing and will not stay with the script as it is written."

When Big Joe heard Mike say that, his face became all red, and the veins began to bulge in his neck. Big Joe says, "Mike, you inform Daniel that if he is unwilling to stick with the script, then I will personally see that he will not every get another leading acting role in any of my future film projects again."

Mike says, "Yes sir, Big Joe; you are the big man. Will there be anything else, sir?"

Big Joe answers, "Yes there is. If you all are not back here by the time that I get back from talking with Floyd about—" Before Big Joe could finish his sentence, the radio goes dead.

Mike sends one of the other crew members over to tell Daniel to communicate what Big Joe had said to tell him.

Now, that was a big mistake on Mike's behalf.

Daniel just sits there for a minute or two, just thinking. His face becomes all red. *Now I should just turn this big truck around and go tell Big Joe a thing or two; but I will not. I will just go to the hospital and check on Susanna.*

At the hospital, there is a security guard who stands about four-foot nothing and who meets Daniel at the door. The security guard says to Daniel in his deep voice, "Sir, how may I help you?"

Daniel replies to the security guard, "Well sir, you see, this nurse who works at Westmore hospital told me that a friend of mine was sent from that hospital over to this hospital, and I am here to check on her."

The security guard takes a deep breath and then asks Daniel, "What is your friend's name?"

Daniel then says to the security guard, "Sir, her name is Susanna."

The security guard then replies, "Susanna what?"

Daniel then takes a step back, scratching his head for a second time, and says, "Oh, no sir, I do not believe that would be my friend's name."

The security guard looks at Daniel with this confused look on his face and says, "No, what is your friend's last name?"

Daniel stops and thinks for a minute and then says, "You know, I never did get what her last name."

Now the film director, in disbelief once again, says to the crew, "I am going to call cut, for this has once again become one big disaster."

That is when the security guard speaks up and says, "Oh no, sir, please do not call cut now, for we were only joking around."

Mike looks over at Daniel and says, "You will be the one who is going to explain to Big Joe why this one scene has taking longer than it should have. Have you forgotten just what he had said about you not staying on script? We don't have much time here."

"Well yes, Mike, I do remember very well what has been said to me by one of the other crew members, now can we just finish this scene and get back to the studio, please?"

As the crew works to get things set in place for the next scene, back at the studio, Big Joe is having this meeting with Floyd about this other screenplay which came across his desk just a week ago. Now Big Joe and Floyd are talking about the screenplay.

Floyd, a screenwriter himself, asked Big Joe, "Just where you get these bizarre screenplays? This one does not seem to make any sense to me at all: here, in this part."

Big Joe says, "Yes, Floyd, I know. It makes no sense to me either. Now Floyd, this particular screenplay was given to me by my wife."

"Oh, Big Joe, I am sorry—I did not know that your wife has started screenwriting."

"It is all good. You see, it was given to her by her brother's wife's sister-in-law, who has this brother-in- law who has a sister whose nephew says a friend of his wrote this book a few years ago about this person who is looking for a new soulmate after going through a nasty divorce."

Floyd looks up from the screenplay at Big Joe and says, "Well, would you like for me to give you my honest opinion?"

"Yes Floyd, I would like to hear your opinion, but before you tell me would you like to get a cup of coffee or a cool soda pop?"

"Well, yes Big Joe, I believe so, after hearing how you came about this bizarre screenplay, but you know, now I am not sure as to which is more bizarre: the story of how you came about it or the screenplay itself."

Big Joe just laughs, and says, "Floyd, which will it be: a cup of coffee or a soda pop?"

"Big Joe, I will have a Ne-hi grape soda."

"Now Floyd, before you give me your opinion, there is something I would like for you to know."

"What would you like me to know, sir?"

"I had Mr. John and his wife Mrs. Mary over the other night, and Mr. John is the one who suggested I have you look and see if you could fill in the blanks."

"Well now, was that not nice of him to suggest that I be the one who you pick."

"Well, Floyd, you are the best screenwriter I have ever had working for me."

"Well, thank you, Big Joe. Now, with that out of the way, am I to guess you are wanting me to see what I can do with this?"

"Yes Floyd, I am asking if you will just take it home with you tonight and read over it once more: see if there's any hope for it."

About that time, Mike and his crew walk in, and they see Big Joe talking with Floyd. Mike walks over to where they are, but before Mike could say anything, Big Joe looks at him and says, "Mike, I will see you all in my office tomorrow morning. Now, Floyd, I am asking you to take that with you and read over it, and if you feel that you need to reword or rewrite any part or parts, please feel free to do so: you have my permission."

"Thank you, sir, I will try my best to see just what it is going to need."

"The End of Scene Two"

That afternoon, Floyd takes the screenplay home with him as Big Joe had asked him to do. After walking through the front door, he sits his briefcase on the coffee table, pulls out the screenplay, pen, and notebook, and sits down on the couch.

As he is reading over the bizarre screenplay, in walks his wife Jimi. She sits down beside him and asks, "Honey, what are you reading?"

Floyd looks up at her and says, "Baby, it is only a bizarre screenplay that Big Joe wants me to see if I can somehow work a miracle on."

"Now honey, what is this bizarre screenplay about?"

Floyd says, "It about this person who had authored this book sometime back. I believe I understood Big Joe to have said a year or two ago."

"Do you know what the book is all about?" Jimi asks.

"From what little I have read of this; I am thinking it is about a person on a quest looking for a new soulmate. Here, you can read it for yourself: I am needing to go to the restroom. But before I go, sweet baby, I gotta tell you: you are looking very sexy tonight, sitting there, wearing that beautiful midnight blue negligee with your legs all curled up on the couch."

"Well, thank you, honey, for those kind words; now, will you just go to the restroom and do your thing?

While I am looking this over, maybe I will be able to help you with it.

"Oh, good you are back now."

"Well Jimi, are you telling me that you miss me? I was only gone for like three minutes."

"No, Floyd, that is not what I meant; now, look, I am thinking if we move this to over here, and put that part here, we just may make this work. What do you think?"

"Now, you may just have something here; yes, you do at that. I sees what you are saying; it sounds better that way."

"Well now, Floyd, just what would you do without me?"

"Hmm. That is a good question; are you sure you would like for me to answer it?"

"Yes, I would, Floyd. Okay, just remember: you are the one who has asked. Now, I am guessing here, but I would just find myself another exceptionally beautiful and hot, sexy secretary who has a great mind like yours."

"Oh, really? Well now, let me tell you this, sweet honey: you just keep thinking that way. When I'm done with you, there is no hot, sexy secretary around here

with a great mind like mine who would ever have anything to do with you, big boy; now that is a fact, Jack."

"Jimi, honey, now you know I was only joking with you. Come on over here, sugar mama, and give your sweet sugar daddy a sweet wet kiss."

"No, Floyd, you just had to go and hurt my feelings, just when, for the first time in an exceedingly long time, when I was all ready to—"

"Wait now, before you say anything else, would it help if I say just how wrong it was for me to have said that? Then I will tell you I'm very sorry. Now, are you going to forgive me and help me with this screenplay so I can take it back to Big Joe tomorrow? You know your baby blue eyes are so beautiful when you get mad."

"Well then, Floyd, if you are wanting me to help you with this after what you just said, it going to cost you big time."

"Oh, Jimi, you know very well that I do not mind the cost. Now, can we get to work on this, Jimi? I am interested in finding out afterwards just what the cost is going to be."

"Now is not the time for you to be thinking about what the cost will be. Your mind needs to be focus on rewriting this screenplay."

"Would you like a glass of tea or a glass of milk before we start?"

"No thank you, Floyd."

"Well, I am going to get me a nice cool beer out of the icebox; I will be right back.

"Okay now, let us get this screenplay done before I fall asleep."

Here is how the screenplay looks after Floyd and Jimi have worked all night to give it a fresh look.

"Scene One"

A circle of people has once again formed inside a coffee shop. They are drinking their coffee and eating snakes at their table.

Jack (35) takes a deep breath. Peter (45) looks over at Jack.

Peter: Are you ready to talk, now Jack?

Jack nods his head and takes another deep breath.

Jack: You know, uh…for I do not know for sure Peter, I just do not know which way I should go in this path which now has been placed before me.

Jack once again shakes his head; he looks defeated.

Jack (cont'd): I now find myself once again to be waiting for my Heavenly Father to provide me with a roadmap, but as it stands for now, Peter, I do not know where I am to go in this world to find my true love who I've been searching for.

Peter: it is all about patience, Jack.

Jack: I know, Peter. Oh, that I do know but I have been waiting for the day when I once again can hold my one true partner, with whom I can share my life with.

Peter: Jack, do you feel that you are now ready for such a commitment?

Jack nods.

Jack: I do believe that I am. I am keeping my faith and truth in Him, and I know He will once again point out the right path for me.

Peter: Yes, you are so right: we should all keep our faith in God, and He will reward us in the end.

Jack: Yes, you are so right we must keep our faith in God.

Well, the very next day, the temperature was once again above ninety-five in Jack's hometown of Waynesboro. Jack calls a few of his friends over to have a backyard cookout. It is a nice sunny day; so, Jack gets out his grill, gets it all ready, and puts on few burgers for his friends. Soon, Rose comes walking up. Jack sees her as a beautiful knockout of a woman and hopes that she is the one he has been waiting for. She smiles at Jack.

Rose: I have been waiting all day just for one of your burger sweeties.

Jack smiles back. Jack: They're ready.

Rose looks over at the grill, turns as she smiles once again at Jack.

Rose: I see the table is ready too, Jack. I prepared lemonade just the way you like it.

She smiles.

Jack smiles.

Jack: Oh, you did; that is nice.

Rose: Yes, Jack, and I might have two more surprises for you as well, honey.

Jack: Yes, what would that be, Rose? Rose only smiles back at Jack.

Jack loses himself in Rose's beautiful baby blue eyes.

Rose sees that he is taken in by her beauty as she stands there smiling. Rose starts to walk away.

Jack tries to follow her, but he is stuck and cannot move an inch.

Jack: Rose!

Jack calls out to Rose, but Rose does not turn around.

INT. JACK'S BEDROOM-NIGHT.

Jack wakes up from a deep dream he just had about Rose. He sighs and puts his hands to his face as frustration becomes clear. He gets up and goes to the shower. After he done taking his shower, he then gets dress for work. As he makes his way to work, he begins to think back to his sweet dream about Rose, wondering if she is the one true love he has been waiting for. On a busy day at the office, Jack is sitting at his office cube, scrolling through paperwork left over from the day before on his computer as he drinks coffee. At the same time, he seems lost in thoughts that he cannot seem, for the life of him, to shake; he looks over the office space. He then looks back down at his computer and opens a new tab; he begins searching for the best spots for a wedding. Beautiful results start coming in, and Jack begins to smile, and then he's interrupted by Little Jimmy (45), who is his boss, who comes walking into his cubicle.

Little Jimmy: Hey, Jack. (beat) How are you doing today? Jack quickly switches the windows back.

Little Jimmy: Now Jack, are you almost done with your work?

Jack: Sure, I am, Little Jimmy. (beat) Well Jack, I see you're a little distracted.

Jack shakes his head. Jack: It is all okay, sir.

Little Jimmy: It better be! Little Jimmy leaves.

Jack sighs.

Jack (V.O): I sit here, thinking deeply about which way this journey may take me in search of my true love.

EXT. PARK-DAY

Jack goes on a walk in the park for his lunch break. He sits on a bench and takes out his lunch. As he begins to eat his steak sandwich, he sees couples who are incredibly happy at the park. There are some walking hand in hand, and there are others hugging, and then there are those who are even kissing. Jack sees them all and he sighs.

Jack (V.O): Now I sit here, trying to figure out the best way to prepare myself for a great journey like this. It appears to be one of the most challenging ones I will ever face in my entire life. (beat) But just knowing within my trembling heart that there could be the most beautiful, loving, God-fearing soulmate somewhere out there, just waiting along that long difficult journey up that one great hill, can only make it become the easiest challenge that I could ever face in this journey.

Jack smiles.

Jack (V.O): Well, maybe, but if I do not try making my way up that hill, then I may never know, will I?

INT. COFFEEE SHOP-DAY

Jack is back at the coffee shop with Peter and the group, talking and laughing. Jack stands up and continues talking.

Jack: Now, as you all may know, I started this journey looking for my one true love only a few years ago, and I must say, I believe today, as I did then, that only God knows just when and where I will meet her.

The group just nods.

Jack goes and stands in line once again at the coffee shop to order a drink. He looks at his watch and realizes it is time for him to head back to work. When he gets to the counter, he orders his coffee. While waiting, Jack scouts the room over to see if he sees Rose.

This beautiful woman enters the shop.

Jack begins to get a little nervous. But soon enough, a man walks in, and it seems he is with the beautiful blue eye's woman. They smile at each other and hold hands. Jack just lowers his head, for he is feeling defeated once again.

Jack (V.O): I shall continue the search through this beautiful but so lonely valley, looking for the one and only wildflower who is also drinking from the living crystal-clear stream of water that provides eternal life with our God.

Jack grabs his coffee and walks out, leaving the group and Peter behind.

EXT. STREET-DAY

Jack is once again on his way to work. As he walks to the officer building, he continues to watch all the happier couples, who are holding each other's hands as they pass him by.

Jack (V.O): Now the search must continue. I must continue moving forward in the living word of God if I am to find an answer in which I am searching for. I find my trembling heart once again feeling very heavy from all the searching for an answer where there may be none. I may never find my one true love ever again.

Jack walks into the office building. Now back at his cubicle, he goes on about his day doing the normal. As Jack's shift ends for the day, he shuts down his computer, stands up, grabs his coat from off the back of the chair, and exits the office.

EXT. STREET-NIGHT

He slowly walks back home, looking tired, but he decides to stop by the coffee shop to see if any of his friends are there. Jack walks into the coffee shop and finds none of his friends there, so he orders another drink, and when he is about to leave, he finds himself locks eyes with a woman as she's entering the coffee shop. She reminds him of Rose.

END OF ACT ONE

Floyd looks at Jimi. "Now, honey, I do not know about you, but I am glad we have finished with this one act of the screenplay."

"Yes Floyd, I agree, but we must sit here and work through the next act."

"Have you looked at the time? it is 9:45, and we both got to be at work tomorrow."

"Yes, I know Floyd, but I have found myself all caught up in getting this bizarre screenplay done. I honestly do believe after we have finished, it is going to turn out to be an unbelievably beautiful love story. Why are you standing up again? Are you going somewhere?"

"No ma'am, I only needed to stretch my legs. Are you sure you want to finish this tonight?"

"Yes, Floyd, I have never been as sure of anything in my life, outside of loving you."

"Well, then I guess I will call Big Joe and ask if I can take tomorrow off.

"Hello, Big Joe, this is Floyd. Sir, the reason for me calling you is to ask if it would be all right with you if I take tomorrow off."

"Why, Floyd, is there something wrong?"

"No sir, there nothing wrong. It just that Jimi and I will be up working all night on this screenplay that you asked me to work on."

"Oh, okay, sure then, I have no problem with that. You can take tomorrow off, but when you are done, I need for you to bring it to my office."

"Okay, Big Joe, thank you, I will do just that. And sir, you have a good night."

"Well, what did he say?"

"He said he is fine with me taking tomorrow off, and he also said that as soon as we are finished, he needs me to bring it to his office."

"Great. Now we can get back work. Well, I first need to get myself a cup of coffee. Oh, I am sorry: would you like one as well?"

"Sure, you can bring me a cup, thank you." Scene One Act Two

INT. JACK'S HOUSE-DAY

The clock on his wall marks the hour right before he must be at work. Jack grabs a chair and sits in front of a little praying space he has in his house. As he begins to pray, he drifts off into this deep, dark, endless dream which takes him on a unique adventure.

INT. JACK'S DEEP, DARK, ENDLESSS DREAM

In this endless dream, Jack finds himself to be in this desolate desert place. He is only there searching for his lovely soulmate. He sees in the far distance what seems to appear to be a caravan of people riding camels. But he finds himself of great thirst and with no strength to call out, so he finds this cactus, takes out his bowie knife, and begins to cut a hole in it. He only gets enough water to wet his parched lips before he falls onto the ground and becomes unconscious. When the caravan of people does find him, he is lying face down. A beautiful goddess of a woman gets down from her camel and walks over to where Jack is lying. She kneels down and turns Jack onto his back and checks to see if he is still alive. She gets up and takes her water from her camel's back and puts a drop or two on his parched lips. When she does,

Jack opens his eyes and he sees an Angel, kneeling over him.

Woman (in a sweet angelical voice): Why are you in this desolate place?

Jack looks up and struggles to speak.

Jack: Before I can answer you, can I please have a drink of your cool water? Then I will tell you.

She gives him a drink of her water.

Jack: You see, I had been on this journey for what seems a lifetime to me as I look for my new soulmate.

The goddess smiles.

Woman: Sir, you seem to be very weak and cannot travel any further out in this desert alone. So, I am going to take you with us back to my father's house, and there I will be able to nurse you back to health.

Jack: I am sorry, but can I ask just who you are? I did not get your name.

She smiles.

Woman: Neither did I get your name.

Jack: Well then, my friends call me Jack. Are you going to tell me your name?

Woman: Jack, my people call me Angela.

Jack: Angela, it is nice to meet you. How far is your father's house from here?

Angela: I would say it may be a two-and-a-half-day ride from here; can you get up on my camel's back by yourself?

Jack: Yes, I think I can, Angela.

Angela: Good, Jack, I would like for us to get another mile or so before it gets dark and we are still able to see how to make camp before nightfall.

Jack looks at his watch and looks back at Angela. Jack: But it is only three o'clock.

Angela: Yes Jack, I know, but out here, nightfall comes exceedingly early. Now, get up here behind me.

Jack gets on the camel's back behind Angela. With the sun still bearing down upon his face, he takes Jane's long silky autumn hair and covers his face and begins to drift off to sleep.

EXT. DESERT-NIGHT

That evening, they found a nice spot to stop and make their camp for the night. Now Jack starts putting up his tent, and as he does so, he starts thinking about Angela and wonders if she could maybe be the love he has been waiting for.

Jack (V.O): But who am I to think that such a beautiful godless woman as her could be the one who could give someone like me everlasting love?

After getting his tent up, he goes looking to find some firewood for the night, and as he does, he notices Angela standing next to her tent. She is wearing this peach-colored blouse slightly below her shoulders, with her silky long autumn hair draped over her left shoulder; he is moved once again by her luscious beauty. She sees him as he is looking over her way and she begins to smile.

Sometime later that evening, Jack is cooking something that he had caught over the campfire he started earlier; Angela waits just before he almost done cooking and walks up and sits down just only a foot or two away from Jack's campfire. They do often look up at each other and smile as Jack is cooking. Jack turns to Angela.

Jack: You know, I have never realized this before until just now Jane: just how beautiful the midnight sky really is at night.

Angela: Why would that be, Jack?

Jack: I will try to answer your question as best as I can. Now, back where I live, there are these things we call streetlights, and when they come on at night, you can barely see the night sky. That is why.

Angela: Well, Jack, that was not so hard for me to understand.

Jack: Well, I guess not, Angela. You are an intelligent person, from what little I do know about you.

Angela: Thank you, Jack.

Jack: Now, Angela, as I was about to say out here: where there are no streetlights, we can see all the bright beautiful stars that appear in heaven. I only wish I could have my motorcycle here with me on this journey.

Angela: Now Jack, I do not mean to sound all dumb now, especially after that nice compliment you gave me, but just what is a motorcycle?

Jack: No, you are not dumb by asking that, but I am more likely the one who is going to sound dumb here, trying to explain what a motorcycle is. I am not sure if you will completely understand all of this, but a motorcycle has only two wheels, one in front and one in the back; it has one set of handlebars and the motor is attached to a frame; the back wheel is turned by either a belt or a chain, and it could either have a long or short seat. That's about all I can tell you about a motorcycle. Maybe one day I can give you a ride on one.

Angela: Now Jack, I might one day like to try riding one, but for now I will pass.

Angela stands up and looks at Jack.

Angela: It has gotten later. I will help you clean the plates.

Once they finished cleaning their plates, Jack looks up at Angela.

Jack: It has been a pleasure talking with you tonight.

Angela: Yes, Jack, it truly has been, but I most now return to my tent. Goodnight, and sweet dreams.

Jack: Thank you, Angela, and the same to you as well.

That very night, as Jack was sleeping, he took Angela's words to heart and begins to dream.

INT. WOODS-DAY

Jack awakens from his slumber and arises to find himself alone in his tent. He steps out of the tent and looks at his surroundings. He finds that Peter and Little Jimmy and everyone else around the camp are gone. He takes a walk down to the lake to see if they are there, but they're not. He then walks back to their campsite, wondering just where they had all gone. He then decided to walk further into the woods to see if they took a walk to find food. As he continues to walk, he spots this beautiful bird sitting on this tree limb chirping away. It sounded like a lovely love song unto Jack, so he finds himself a place to sit and listens as the bird chirps it loves song. As he listens, he remembers this time long ago, when he first met the loveliest young lady he had ever laid eyes on. The way she smiled made his heart flutter like a butterfly flapping its wings for the very first time as it tries to fly from its cocoon. She lived in his hometown, Waynesboro. He recalls their very first date that, and the restaurant he had taken her to after the movie that they enjoyed watching. They had sat holding hands for the first time, and even their very first kiss, as he recalls, was a short, fast one, for they were both very nervous; they had never kissed anyone other than their parents, and even then only on the cheek. Right before his dream could reach its ending, Angela woke him, asking him if he was ready to continue their long journey unto her father's house. Jack looks up at her and nods his head. A great amount of time has passed after leaving their camp. Jack then begins telling Angela about his bizarre dream that he was having when she awoke him that morning. As he is telling her about his bizarre dream, she begins to tear up a little. He sees her beautiful eyes as they begin to form tears.

Jack: Angela, why do you have tears coming down your sweet rosy cheeks?

Angela finds herself trying to answer Jack, and at the same time she is fighting back her emotions.

Angela: Jack, as I was listening to you tell me about your dream, I started to remember my very first date as well.

Before she could even say anything to Jack about her first date, he was awoken by his phone. It was Little Jimmy, asking why he did not show up for work today. Jack tells her that he had fallen back to sleep and had this bizarre dream about being on a journey looking for his soulmate.

INT. RESTAURANT-DAY

Well, the next day was Saturday, Jack's day off from work. He wakes up from his slumber and takes a walk down to the coffee shop, where he finds himself meeting up with Rose.

Jack says hello and asks if she would like to join him for a meal.

Rose looks at him.

Rose: Yes, I would love to, Jack. Jack smiles.

Jack: Rose, are you sure you want to be seen with me? Angela just nods.

Jack feels reassured.

Jack (V.O.): She is one of a kind. Someone like her is hard to find in today's world. O Lord my God, I pray that You will keep me on the right path that You have laid out before me to continue this travel in search of my beloved soulmate. Thank You oh Lord my God, for Your many blessings, in which I feel that I do not so deserve.

INT. LOBBY-DAY

After finding a book at this bookstore. Jack and Rose walk up to a man whose name Ricardo.

Jack: Hi.

Ricardo only smiles.

Jack points to the picture of a boat in the book.

Ricardo smiles again as he tries to follow what Jack is trying to ask him. But Ricardo does not fully understand what is being asked of him.

Jack turns and asks Rose if she minds trying to see if Ricardo could understand her better.

Angela: Jack, I'm sure he understood you. Jack has a confused look on his face.

Jack: Rose, how can you be so sure?

EXT. DESERT-DAY

They went out for a walk along the beach. Jack turns and looks at Angela.

Jack: Looks as if we are going to be waiting for an exceedingly longer time than what we had expected.

Angela: Why?

Jack: Well, until the ship carrying the shipment of supplies comes in.

He takes a deep breath.

Jack: Let us find a place to stay until then.

Angela: Okay then, I'll go this way and you can go down that way. If either of us finds a place before the other does, we can return here and wait until the other shows up.

As she tells Jack this, he finds himself hypnotized by her beautiful blue eyes. He tries to shack it off.

Jack: Okay, I am fine with that.

Later that day, Jack walks into a lobby.

INT. LOBBY-DAY

He sees Angela sitting at this table, talking with this much younger man, and he stops, and he reddens as he gets jealous. Angela laughs at the man's joke. Jack cannot move a muscle, for he can only observe them laughing.

Jack (V.O): I cannot even begin to find the words within myself to tell Angela that I have these extraordinarily strong feelings for her, the kind that I never felt for a beautiful woman like her in my entire life.

As he stands there only watching her, she just sits there at the table with this much younger man, talking and laughing. He tries to divert his thoughts from her by looking back at his schooldays as a young man.

INT. SCHOOLDAYS FLASHBACK SCENE

In a small, crowded classroom, a younger Jack is in school. Jack finds he has received a bad grade on one of his homework papers. He looks down and becomes embarrassed, for the people sitting next to him are laughing.

Jack (V.O): I have always struggled with my self-esteem. He takes a breath.

Jack (V.O): I feel as if I do not always fit in because of my inability to learn things like others do so easily. I feel as if people will always be looking down on me, because they all may be thinking that I am not as capable of being as smart as they are. That I can't read or write like everyone else does. Now that I have gotten older in life, it does not seem to matter what people say about me as it once did, for I know within my heart the great true love of my God, and that is all that matters to me.

END FLASHBACK SCENE.

EXT. OCEAN/ BEACH-DAY

Jack once again finds himself all alone sitting on the beach, while he is still in this deep endless dream of his.

Jack (V.O): I look out across the great ocean, seeing if there is a ship coming in at this time of day. I don't see a single one coming in.

Jack looks back down and shakes his head.

Jack (V.O): I am feeling down and discouraged about the way my journey has turn out so far, but I must take my faith in my God, for only He knows the true outcome of my life journey. Although my faith is with Him, I am finding this to be one of the hardest roads to travel out of all those which I have traveled.

Jack turns once more to the sky and looks for a sign from Him.

INT. Jack's HOUSE-DAY

Jack (V.O): Years earlier, I carried this smile upon mine face as I walked into my house after work one day. There, a cake sat on the kitchen table: my wife Cynthia had not forgotten it was my birthday. She meets me as I start down the hallway, going to our bedroom to change my clothes. She had a frown upon her beautiful face, which I had not seen in such a long time.

Jack: What is wrong with you, honey? Why do you have a frown on your beautiful, sweet face?

Cynthia looked at Jack.

Cynthia: I am sorry.

Cynthia takes a deep breath.

Cynthia: Jack, I have tried everything that I could think of, but I just cannot be with you any longer; I feel within my heart that there is no love for you any longer.

Jack pales.

Jack: But Cynthia, it is my birthday. Now, of all days, you feel like this is the one you must tell me that you're no longer in love with me?

Cynthia: Now look Jack, I know it hard for you to understand this, and it is hard for me to tell you as well, but I just can no longer be with you as your wife. I feel no love for you, like I once did when we first met twenty- five years ago.

Jack grows bewildered as she says this.

Jack (V.O): I could only think: just how is it even possible to up and stop loving someone after all these years together, taking care of each other's needs through the best of times and the worst of times. She is right: I cannot begin to understand how this could even be possible. It is a question to which I know no answer, even at this stage in my life.

INT. LAWYER OFFICE-DAY.

Jack (V.O): Cynthia and I are sitting in front of a lawyer, and we sign our divorce papers. Neither she nor I could look each other in the eye, not even to say that it had been nice while it lasted. That day, I felt as if my life had come to an end, for the one I was in love with had taken my heart right out from within me. Today, I am looking forward to when the supply ship will arrive. My journey must be moving on down this ole rugged road I call life. See, I must continue to search for my beautiful soulmate. I feel within my heart that she is out there, somewhere in this old world, just waiting for me to come walking into her life. I honestly cannot say just when or where that time will be. For now, seems unlikely and impossible for me to find my way to her.

EXT. OCEAN/BEACH-DAY

Jack finds himself to be back at the beach once again.

Jack (V.O): As I am sitting here today alone. Just looking out across the beautiful crystal-clear blue ocean, I remember a time when my stepdad took us to this river that once had a place where you could go swimming. I was only a young boy, only four or five at that time, who had not learned how to swim. Well, I go walking into the water alone with the rest of the family. As I kept walking, the water kept getting deeper. I found myself crawling up my step-sister's back. You may think that to be funny, seeing me crawling up her back the way I did. Well, we both would've drowned that day if she had not known how to swim. Because of that incident, to this day, I am not that fond of being submerged in water. Therefore, I am praying that the ship I might find myself to be on leaving this desert does not spring any big leak, for this old boy cannot swim or walk on water.

END OF ACT TWO ACT THREE

After leaving the lobby where Jack saw Angela earlier that afternoon, talking and laughing with another man, Jack is feeling now as if there is no hope that Angela has any interest in him like he's interested in her.

EXT. OCEAN/BEACH-NIGHT

As Jack finds himself once again to be walking on the beach, he becomes a little calmed by the sound of the waves and starts to think things over in a much clearer way.

Jack's (V.O): As I continue my walk along this beautiful ocean, I am having a conversation with my Lord about this situation in which I have now found myself to be in with Angela. As I am talking with my God, I turn to look out upon the ocean, for the moon has now reached a perfect position to reflect its great light upon the beautiful crystal-clear blue ocean. I find it to be so peaceful and beautiful out here tonight that I could lie down right here and try counting the stars in heaven's beautiful night sky. I see them as trying to show me this roadmap as to where I am to travel next in my journey of life. I then take a deep breath and slowly exhale; there seems to be all these turns which I should be taking alone in this search to find my only true lovely soulmate. I find it to be odd though, in a way, for it seems as if they are showing me there may be no end to my life journey or any hope in ever finding her. I feel now within my heart, from having a talk with my God, who knows all things, that I must wait upon Him, for He is teaching me that those who wait upon Him will grow stronger in their faith in Him and will one day reach the plan He has laid out for them. As I am getting closer to the house that Angela and I had found to stay at while we are waiting until the supply ship returns, I see her sitting outside on the steps of the front porch with her chin in her hands. It appears like she is in deep thought about something. I smile and just sit down next to her. I look over at her.

Jack: It is a beautiful moon shining tonight. Angela does not even look up at me.

Angela: Why did you would up and leave me here all alone tonight, Jack?

I look at her and become a little nervous, because I didn't know just how I was going to answer her.

Jack: Angela, I thought you may have had something else you needed to do tonight.

Angela: Well, Jack did you not stop and think that, just maybe, I too would have loved to take a moonlight walk and see its lovely reflection on the ocean and the stars as well? It has all ways been a dream of mine, to one day going down to the ocean on a night like this one and just sit on the sand and watch the waves as they come in and go back out under the moonlight.

Jack: Angela, I would love for you and me, if you so wish, to take that walk right now?

Angela begins to blush and has little smile.

Angela: Oh, yes, I would love to take a walk in the moonlight with you down to the ocean and just sit there on the beach, watching all those waves as they are moving under this beautiful moonlit starry night.

EXT. OCEAN/MOONLIGHT-WALK

Jack: Angela, there is something I would like to say to you, if you do not mind me saying it.

Angela: What is on your mind?

Jack: Angela, I am glad we are sitting out here on the beach together tonight.

Angela: Now, Jack, by the look you have in your eyes, I believe you to have more than that on your mind.

Jack: Yes Angela, I do: do you remember the day which you found me out here in this desolate stretch of desert?

Angela: Yes, Jack, I remember.

Jack: Now, Angela, I am not good at explaining my feelings to anyone, so I hope you understand what I am trying to tell you when I say that I feel as if I am falling in love with you. Why are you blushing? Did I just say something that I should not have said?

Angela: Oh, no, Jack, you did not say anything wrong., It's just I did not know you were starting to feel that way about someone like me.

Jack: Well, you are an unbelievably beautiful lady, and I would love one day to be able to call you my wife.

Angela: Wait now Jack, I am afraid you are getting a little ahead of yourself here.

Jack: Why's that, Angela?

Angela: Jack, there is so little that you know about me, and I am afraid once you find out more about me, you will feel different and become hurt again.

Jack (V.O): As we walk back to the house, I look down at Angela's hand, not sure if I should take her hand in mine as I continue to admire her beauty. I wonder what she may be thinking about me, after I had opened my big dumb mouth and told her I was falling head-over-heels in love with her. She's got to be thinking that I am the dumbest person she has ever met. Once we get back, I say good night.

Angela smiles.

Angela: Jack, I like you, and I did enjoy our walk tonight and I hope you have a good night's sleep.

Jack and Angela then go to their only room. INT. LOBBY-DAY

Jack (V.O): I pour myself a nice hot cup of coffee to start the day off, as I always do. As I am drinking my coffee, Linda walks up.

Jack: Good morning, Linda, have you by any chance seen Angela this morning? When you went by her room or came down the stairs just now?

Linda: Yes, Jack, I did, and she told me that she was going into town to do a little shopping with one of her new guy friends that she had met.

Jack: Well, do you know just how long she's been gone?

Linda: Oh, I would say two hours at the most; now, why do you ask?

Jack: There is no reason, Linda; I was only curious about her whereabouts, for I had not seen her this morning. If you have no plans for the day, would you mind going into town with me?

Linda: Sorry Jack, but I do have plans to work on my school paper I need to turn in on Monday morning.

Jack: Well thanks Linda; I guess I can make a go at it alone.

EXT. TOWN-DAY

Jack (V.O): I walk about the streets of this small, busy town, looking for Angela. I look in all the stores and I do not find her in any of them. As I continue my search for her, I smell food cooking. I start to look to see if I could find where the food is being cooked, for I did not take time to eat before starting my search for Angela this morning, and now I have become hungry. I find a small café on the street corner and I go in and make my order.

EXT. OUTDOOR EATING AREA-DAY

Jack (V.O): After I get my food, I find a table outdoors to eat. As I am eating, I look up and see Angela walking into the café with the young man who she had met back at the lobby a week or so earlier. Angela sees me sitting at the table and she only smiles; she and the guy she is with go on in and order they food. Later, she comes and joins me, and we sit there eating our meal.

Jack: There seems to be a vessel coming in, but it will be three to five days or so before it makes it way to the dock.

Angela: I see.

Jack (V.O): As we are finishing our meal together, for the life of me, I cannot take my eyes off her. God, only You know the true answer to this question of my fading heart. Why does her beauty seem to hypnotize me every time we are all alone? I only know this much: I can come unto You and lay it all into Your hands. You, my God, have always been right by my side to guide me alone the way, and no matter what may come between Angela and me, I believe you to have my best interests at heart.

EXT. OCEAN/BEACH-DAY

Jack (V.O): I find myself once again all alone, walking down by the ocean. I find this place to sit and contemplate the beauty of the waves as they come and go, but just where they go, I do not know. As I am watching them coming and go, I begin to write into my little notebook a few of my deep inner thoughts. Oh,

Lord if it is not in Your will for Angela and me to become friends any longer, will You please once and for all just take her out of my mind, for I do not know if I am going to make it. My Lord, only You understand why she has found her way into my life. The other day, as she sashayed into the room where I was sitting, drinking a cool glass of lemonade, her beauty took my breath away, leaving me speechless. As I write down my deepest inner thoughts, my eyes begin to close, and I once again start to have this dream.

INT. JACK's BEDROOM-DAY

Jack (V.O): I hear someone knocking at my bedroom door.

Angela: Jack, are you up? It is time to leave this place.

Jack (V.O): I jump up, pack up my things, and run out the door as if I'd been shot out of a cannon.

INT. LOBBY-DAY

Jack (V.O): I make my way down to the lobby. Once there, I see Angela. She smiles and I return the smile; I then walk over to where she is standing.

Angela: Well, Jack, I guess this will be the last time we see each other.

Jack (V.O): When I heard her say those words, my head begins to slowly drop with sadness. I then take a deep breath and look away so she doesn't see the tears form in my eyes from the pain of those words. After I had regained my composure, I then reach into my bag and take out some things, and then turn back, facing her once again and giving them to her.

Jack: Angela, I hope these will one day remind you of me in the days to come, and that you will also remember those words which I told you on that moonlit night as we walked along the ocean. As for me, Angela, I promise you that I will never forget the beautiful song you had sung that night. With the sound of your sweet angelic voice that night, it seemed like the waves stopped in mid-air, as though they were listening to your song.

Jack's (V.O): I am not sure, as I am leaving here, if those items which I have given her will have the right effect on such a special sweet lady as her. I am beginning to feel my trembling heart as I walk away from her for the last time, leaving this beautiful, sweet lady behind. I am reminded of that one sweet, lovely dream I once had may not have been meant for her. But, for a reason unknown to me, I felt a strong need within myself to present them to her just the same, if only to see what her reaction would be. The day has finally come: the ship which I have been patiently waiting upon is arriving. In what seems like a lifetime ago for me, I am now ready to set back out onto the open sea which it comes from. I stand here, waiting to board the ship; I can only wonder if she is going to join me or not. Now, will it only be me starting this new journey on the open sea, where the waves come and go, but just where to, one knows not? Before I do get aboard this ship, I feel a great need to take one last look for her. I only see that she is nowhere to be found, and my eyes once again form tears like the water in this great ocean. I find that the only thing I have left of her to hold onto is her beautiful, innocent smile, engraved within my lonely heart. I am now about to depart upon this great journey, which may one day lead me to my sweet, awaiting soulmate. But until that day comes, I find myself beginning alone once again, only to be holding my deepest inner love for Angela to myself, for I am unable to share it with her.

Jack boards the ship to start what he feels to be a new beginning to his search, for his one true love. The Captain announces that there will be a great delay in their departure. Jack drops his head once again in disbelief. He goes to find The Captain to ask why there is going to be a great delay.

The Captain: There is a humongous hurricane brewing in the ocean, and it is within the path which we would be traveling; and I was informed that we must remain docked here until the hurricane has passed.

Jack: Sir, were you told how long you must wait?

The Captain: Look now, Jack, if you don't know anything at all about hurricanes, I will tell you that they are very unpredictable; now, if you do not mind, I got work do.

Jack: Oh, Captain, sir, there is one more thing I would like to ask of you.

The Captain: Well, what will that be?

Jack: Captain, will you please be sure to let me know as soon as we are ready to depart?

The Captain: Now, Jack, I will ensure you are the very first person I let know. Now, I'm going to ask you for the last time to debark my vessel.

Jack shakes his head and then exits the vessel, only to find himself back in his living room, where this bizarre dream started. Jack begins to rub his eyes as he looks up at the clock on the wall; it shows five minutes before the hour he must be at work. He picks up the phone and calls his boss Little Jimmy.

Jack: Hello sir, this is Jack. I am calling you, sir, to inform you I am going to be an hour late getting to work today.

Little Jimmy: Well, okay, Jack, I do appreciate you calling to let me know.

Little Jimmy hangs up.

Little Jimmy (V.O): Now why am I the one who must put up with someone like Jack?

Little Jimmy starts to question himself.

Little Jimmy (V.O.): Now, what great wrong did I do today to get be punished like this? I may never know the answer to this question.

THE END

Floyd jumps up and says, "Jimi honey, I do believe we have reached the end of this bizarre screen play!"

"Yes, Floyd, we have, I hope when you take it to Big Joe tomorrow, he will like It after all this challenging work."

It is sometime around five o'clock at Floyd's home. He gets up and goes to shower before getting ready to start his workday. While he is taking his shower, he also shaves, and he starts to wonder if there a song could be written for the screenplay. *I'll just ask Big Joe when I get to work.*

Once Floyd gets dressed, he goes over to the bed, where Jimi is laying, leans over, whispers in her ear, and then gives her a kiss. "Honey, I will see you when I get home tonight."

Jimi, still feeling sleepy from being up, turns onto her back, stretching her arms outwards, and says, "I love you too. Have a wonderful day, and I will see you later when you get home."

Jimi then gets up at six and goes to the shower. After she is done, and as she is blow-drying her hair, she starts to wonder, *What outfit am I going to wear to work today?* She is thinking of wearing her new low-cut red tank-top that she bought last week and blue jeans with red ankle-high heels.

After getting dressed, she heads off to work.

Floyd has made his way to the studio. He enters Big Joe's office at about 7:30 a.m. He walks up to the secretary's desk and asks Anna, Big Joe's wife, if he is in his office.

She answers, "No Floyd he is not. When we got here this morning, he said he needed to go over and check on Mike's film over at Morehead hospital."

"Now, Anna, are you telling me that Mike has not finished that film yet?"

Anna just looks at Floyd and says, "You do realize who he has working as the lead actor, right?"

Floyd nods and smiles, turns, and starts walking back toward the door. He stops and looks back at Anna.

Anna sees that he is looking back at her and asks, "Floyd, is there something else I can help you with?"

"Well, yes there is this one thing."

"Well, spit it out man; I do not have all day!"

"As you can see, Jimi and I are finally done with the screenplay that Big Joe had asked me to work on, and I was wondering if could have a theme song written for it."

Anna smiles and nods. "Yes, Floyd, but Big Joe said that he was not going to say anything until he was sure you were able to give it a makeover."

Floyd smiles and nods.

Anna says, "Floyd, you got me curious: why you would ask about the screenplay having a theme song?"

Floyd once again smiles. "Anna, when I was taking my shower this morning, I started thinking that if I had the book which this screenplay was written from, or a song, then I feel like Jimi and I could have done more for it."

Anna says, "thinking ofo, are you thinking doing it like this movie called…" Anna pauses, taking a deep breath, "now what is the name of that movie?"

Floyd looks at her with a funny look on his face and asks, "What movie are you thinking of?"

Anna says, "Oh, Floyd, the one which use Kenny Rogers' song—The Gambler!"

When Anna says that, Floyd just could not help but to burst out into laughter. Floyd, still laughing, turns away, trying to get his composure.

"Now, why are you laughing at me?"

Floyd turns back and says, "Anna, I am sorry; I could not hold it back. If you could have seen the expression on your face as you were thinking of the name of the movie The Gambler, you would be laughing too."

Anna says, "So you find my expression to be funny. You should have seen the one on Mike's face when Big Joe told him he'd been pranked by his own crew the day before."

"Well, Anna, I wish I could have been here to see it. I know it was a big shocker for Mike," Floyd says. "Thank you for the information; I will come by later to see Big Joe about this bizarre screenplay."

"Okay then, Floyd, you have a wonderful day."

Floyd answers, "You as well." He turns and walks out.

Anna says, "Oh wait, Floyd, when you talk with Big Joe, please do not tell him I told you about the theme song."

Floyd nods and smiles and exits the office.

Daniel is at the hospital and is now checking on Susanna, who is sitting up in bed, eating lunch.

Daniel walks in, sits down on the couch, and starts talking to her. He asks what the doctor has said about her head.

She answers, "Well, as of now, the doctor has not come by to let me know anything."

Daniel sits back on the couch and asks if it would be alright to watch the television.

"Sure, Daniel, so long as we watch 'Days of our Lives' and not of those old Westerns that you like to watch."

Daniel smiles. "Well, alright then."

About a half-hour passes, and in walks Dr. James T. Morehead. "The T. is short for Thomas," he says as he introduces himself for the first time to Susanna and Daniel. "Susanna, I understand that you were transferred here for a head injury: is that correct, young lady?"

"Well now, Dr. James T. Morehead, that is what they had told me, so I believe it to be true."

"Wait now, I am sorry if the way I said that came across sounding as if I was being a ----------. I was only trying to assess just how serious your condition is today. Now, Susanna, can you tell me how you received your injury?"

Susanna, still suffering memory loss, looks at him and answers, "No sir, I am not sure I know."

The doctor asks, "Now, just what do you remember about your accident?"

"Well, Doctor, what I do remember is fuzzy."

Daniel speaks up and starts to say something, and the doctor stops him, saying, "Sir, I need her to answer my questions, not you." The doctor looks back at Susanna after telling Daniel to keep his mouth shut and asks, "Can you tell who this guy is?"

Susanna takes a breath and answers, "He told me his name is Daniel."

"Well, is Daniel your husband?"

Susanna looks at Daniel for a second or two, then looks back at the doctor. "Sir, I do not believe I know just who he really is, and I most definitely do not believe him to my husband."

The doctor then says, "Okay. Susanna, I would like to speak with him outside the door, for just a minute, and we'll be right back."

So, they step out, and the doctor tells Daniel about just how serious her memory loss is, and then they walk back into Susanna's room.

The doctor begins to tell Susanna that she has what they call amnesia. "Only a minor version, from what I've seen from your CT scan; now, Susanna, I do not want you to get alarms at what I'm fixing to tell you, but I've also seen where you had a little bleeding at one point. The good news is it was not so severe that I feel the need to do surgery. Although, with all of that said, I do feel that you need to stay another day or two, just to be sure the bleeding does not start up again. I will stop by to check in on you sometime tomorrow. Now please, get your rest, young lady."

Susanna says, "Wait, doctor, is there anything that you can give me to help me sleep?"

"Sure, young lady, I'll have one of the nurses give you a prescription that should help you rest better."

An hour passed before the nurse brings Susanna her shot of medicine. As the nurse comes walking in, Daniel stands up and tells Susanna that he would be back tomorrow to see her.

As he starts to leave Susanna's room, she reaches out her hand and takes his, saying, "Daniel, you are not going to leave me all alone here, are you?"

He takes a step next to her bed, then leans over and kisses her on the forehead, and says, "Susanna, I got to finish this film before Mike has me fired."

"Well, Daniel if you must go, then just go, but please promise me you will be back tomorrow."

Daniel then nods and exits the room.

He makes a stop down at the nurses' station and asks them if they would please take diligent care of Susanna, for she is his only reason to live, and then he exits the hospital.

Once they finally finished filming their last scene at the hospital, Mike informs his crew to start packing everything up to head back to the studio for the final scene.

END OF ACT THREE

Big Joe has called Floyd to bring over the bizarre screenplay. Floyd picks up his handmade brown leather briefcase and starts walking over to Big Joe's office.

As Floyd is walking in, Anna looks up and says, "Look now Floyd, you are not to say anything about me telling you that there is a theme song, right?"

Floyd nods and smiles. "Is he in?"

"Sure Floyd, you can go on in: he is waiting for you."

Floyd picks back up his briefcase and takes it in with him into the meeting.

"Good afternoon, Floyd, have a seat."

Floyd sits down and puts his briefcase in his lap. "So, Floyd, do you have the screenplay in there?"

"Yes, sir. I must tell you that Jimi would not let me go to bed until we had finished this bizarre screenplay."

"Well, Floyd, let me have a look at it and see what kind of work you both have done."

Floyd opens his briefcase, pulls out the screenplay, and hands it over to Big Joe. Big Joe starts to flip through it.

Floyd says. "Sir, as I was on my way here this morning. I was thinking if this bizarre screenplay could have a theme song."

"Why would you be thinking something like that, Floyd?"

"Well, sir, as you well know, I have no knowledge of this person's background, so as Jimi and I rewrote it, I couldn't help but feel that if we had known a little bit about the person, it would have made it easier trying to fill in all the blanks. That, sir, is why I was wondering."

"Oh, I think I understand what you are telling me. You are saying that if you had something more to collaborate with, you feel that you could have done a better job: now, am I right?"

"Yes, you understood me all right."

Big Joe smiles and says, "Floyd, I did not say anything to you Monday because I was hoping you could make this work as it is. The theme song is just as bizarre. Now, if you are still wanting to see it, I can call Anna and ask her to bring it in."

"Yes sir, I would definitely would like to see how close we came to matching them together."

"Well, Floyd, just from what I am seeing here, you and Jimi have once again done an outstanding job. Now let me see if Anna is still at her desk.

Big Joe thinks, *That hot, sexy lady*, as he pushes the button on the intercom to ask Anna to bring in the theme song for Floyd.

Anna replies, "Yes sir, I'll be right in with it."

She arises from behind her desk and walks over to the filing cabinet, pulls out a drawer, gets the theme song marked, "My Beautiful, Lonely Wildflower," and carries it into where Floyd is sitting. She is smiling, when she hands it to him; Floyd smiles back as he is nods. Big Joe just happens to look up as they are smiling at each other. Anna returned to her desk before Big Joe could question her about why she has a big smile on her face. Floyd looks over the theme song for the first time today.

"My Beautiful Wildflower Song"

Verse 1: I was waiting for my dream to come, full of hope, full of love. The wildflowers hear my song of the girl with the innocent brown eyes. The heavens made us meet. My heart is so troubled I cannot speak. For the sweet soft petals of my tender heart and the wind caressing your cheek.

Chorus: Oh, so long ago, walking down that old, rugged road beyond the cliff, above the valley, swaying softly as the wind blows. You are my only wildflower…yeehaw.

Verse 2: Going back to the memories I knew, I remember the promise I said to you. She is my only one in the fields of many growing wild, my wildflower the girl with an innocent smile. A long journey that was a while, as the rain drops gently in my heart, I knew.

Chorus: Oh, so long ago, walking down that old, rugged road. We traveled to escape the desert and waited for the ships to sail with you. Oh, my wildflower.

Bridge: It all feels just like a dream now. The winds blow harder, burning bridges wide awake. It seemed like forever was gone (my wildflower). Watching the smoke dwindling behind me. This journey I have to go alone, I see the petals of the young wildflower now; it felt like only a figment of my own (my wildflower).

Chorus: Oh, so long ago, walking down that old, rugged road, above the cliff, beyond the valley, swaying softly as the wind blows. My wildflower… Oh, so long ago walking down that old, rugged road. We traveled to escape the desert and waited for the ships to sail with you (My Wildflower)

"Well, Floyd, what are your thoughts? Do you see where it could have helped you any?"

"Well, first, let me say you were right: this song is as bizarre as the screenplay, and that was before Jimi redid most of it. But to be honest with you, Big Joe, I can only wonder just what the person who wrote this song must have been thinking at the time, and I will say, from the sound of it, they may been even drinking a little something stronger than coffee, if you know what I mean. Now Big Joe, I can't think of a single singer who might would be interested in trying out this song."

"Floyd, I was wondering the same thing, but there's got to be someone looking to try out a new song like this one."

"Well, good luck finding someone who is willing to try this bizarre song. Now, will there be anything else before I go that you may need me to do?"

Is Floyd thinking that we should rewrite this bizarre song? "No, Floyd, I do believe that is all for now, but if you happen to see Mike, tell him I need to see him."

"Yes, sir. I will let him know."

"Oh, Floyd do not forget now to tell Jimi how much I do appreciate her helping you with the screenplay. You both have done a fantastic job. Now, my job is I got to somehow convince Mike to take it and turn into a great movie."

"Now, I am sorry, Big Joe, did you just say something to me?"

"No, Floyd, I was only thinking aloud here, but as you leave, will you tell Anna to step in here? I'm going to have her to run this song out and just see if someone is willing to try it."

"Anna, Big Joe asked me to tell you: he needs to see you."

Mike and his crew return from filming over at the hospital. Mike tells his lead crew member to watch things while he takes the film over to the editor to have the film edited for Thursday's presentation. On his way, he sees Floyd coming from Big Joe office. He walks over to where Floyd is and asks how the screenplay turned out.

"Well, Mike, I do believe it came out surprisingly good. Big Joe willing was impressed with the way it looked, and speaking of Big Joe, he asked me to tell you he needs to see you in his office."

Did he, by any chance, say why he needs to see me?"

"No, Mike, he did not say why. Now, how did the film turn out for you?"

"Well, once Big Joe told Daniel face-to-face that if he did not stay on script, he would let him go, it all went very well. I was on my way over to have it edited for Thursday's big presentation."

"Mike, if you do not mind, I will take it over to the editor for you; when Big Joe told me to tell you he needs you in his office, he sounded as if he meant *now.*"

Mike drops his head and says, "Oh well," and hands the film rolls over to Floyd. Mike, shaking his head, wonders as he slowly walks toward Big Joe's office: *Just what could I have done for him needing to see me?*

As he walks in, Anna is sitting at her desk, tapping her foot to a song she is listening to on her headset, and did not hear Mike come in.

Mike, in a deep voice, says, "Excuse me, Anna, I do not mean to interrupt all the demanding work you are doing, but is Big Joe in his office? Floyd said he needs to see me."

"Yes, Mike, he is in his office, but! You're going to have to wait! He is on the phone with a new singer."

Mike nods and takes a seat by the door. After ten minutes or more pass, Big Joe gets off the phone, opens the door, and asks Mike to step into the office.

Mike gets up and proceeds into the office, saying, "Now, Big Joe, I'd like for you to know that whatever is wrong, I did not have anything do with it: I am just telling you upfront."

Big Joe started laughing so hard as Mike was saying that that he almost missed his chair. "Oh no, Mike, there is nothing wrong. I have asked to see you now because I have a new project for you."

"Oh, I was thinking from the way Floyd just told me ten minutes ago that you were needing to see me in your office, like yesterday. It made me think that something was seriously wrong."

"Mike, you know Floyd likes to exaggerate things. Now, back to this new project I have for you: you recall the screenplay that Floyd rewrote for me, right?"

"Yes, Sir, I do, for he and I were just talking about when he told me you wanted to see me."

"Did he also tell you, Mike, that I believe with your talent and your knowledge of knowing how to get things done, you could make this into one of the biggest movies in your lifetime?"

"Wow, I did not see that coming. But thank you, Big Joe, for having confidence in me. Please do not take what I am about to say in the wrong way, because I do appreciate everything you just said, but do you feel like you lay it on a little thick?"

"Well, Mike I was only trying to convince you, in such a way that you might would like to take on the job."

"Well, may I take it home and study it over for, say, a week or two?"

"Now, Mike, what if I say more like a day or two?"

"Come now, Big Joe, let us get back to reality here: you know we still have the big presentation coming up Thursday, right, and there's work in getting that project over with?"

"Yeah, you're right, I guess. I will give you a week to decide if you would like to do the job or not."

"Big Joe, I might as well ask: are you wanting Daniel to be the lead actor, because if you are, I will go ahead and tell you, I do not think that I will be doing this job?"

"Wait, hold on here now, Mike. Before you go making any wrong decisions here about this film, I know Daniel can at times be hard to work with—we both know that, right?"

"Yes sir, Big Joe."

"Good, we both agree. Would you say that Daniel has ways to make the hardest scenes work out to his advantage, compared to others actor that we know could?"

"Well, he does at that, but Big Joe, he also has this crazy was of thinking of himself as being always right, even when he knows he is wrong. Now, take for instance this one scene at Westmore hospital, and the one where he was pulled over by the highway patrol. Now, Big Joe, do not forget the final scene where he was joking around with the security guard at Morehead hospital."

"Now, I do understand your frustration with Daniel, but you know I will have your back all the way on this project, and I will even go as far as to let you pick out your own female leading actor for this film, since Susanna is going to be out for some time. Now, Mike, what do you say?"

"Well, Big Joe, if I do direct this film for you, and I am not saying I will, but the very first time Daniel goes off script, I am finished, and that is all I going to say on this subject."

"Mike, I am sorry you feel that way. Now, if not Daniel, then just who would you prefer me choose?"

"Well, Big Joe, after I've had time to read and study the screenplay, I feel I could give you an answer. Are you good with that, sir?"

"Yes, Mike, I'm good with that."

The End

"Now, Clay, just what have you been doing in you room all day?"

"Mrs. Mary, I have been trying to write what I call a screenplay, but I am finding it to be a great challenge."

"Whatever gave you the idea that you could write a screenplay?"

"Mrs. Mary, I did not say that I *could* write one; what I said was I *trying* to see if could, and what gave me that idea was no other than Mr. John."

"Clay, just when did John ever give you an idea like that?"

"Mrs. Mary, you recall when he said he was going to take you to watch one, and he said it sounded just like something I would one day write about?"

"Yes, I do remember Clay. Now if you do not mind, I would like to see just what you have written."

"Mrs. Mary, I was kinda hoping you would take a look at it for me and give me feedback."

"Clay, I would be happy to read over it for you."

"Yes, ma'am, let me go and print it off for you, and I will be right back.

"Mrs. Mary, where did you go?"

"Clay, I am in the living room, sitting on the couch."

"Here is what I have so far."

Mrs. Mary begins to read what I have written, and it appears that she is incredibly surprised about it. She says, "Clay, from what I just read here, you may have a delightful story going, but I am not sure if I would call it a screenplay."

"Well, why is that? Is there something wrong with it?"

"Oh, no, Clay it's not that at all: it needs more information in places, I guess you might say. Now, Clay, if you like for me to, I'd be more than happy to ask John if he would see if Big Joe might would look at it when you're done."

"You really think it's that good?"

"Clay, if I did not think it was any good, you know I would have told you so, for I am not like John."

"Thank God you are not anything like John, Mrs. Mary.
He is always telling me I am dumb."

"Now, Clay, do not go selling yourself short just because he says that. I feel he doesn't really mean it. I must ask before you go: what all are of these EXT., INT., and (Cont'd), (Beat)—what are they about? I don't understand why you are using them."

"Mrs. Mary, it is my understanding that they're used to show the actors what they are to do next in the scene."

"Well, okay, Clay, if that is what you say they used for, I guess I can live with it."

"Now, Mrs. Mary, I have a question for you: just how far have you gotten into my writing?"

"I have read to where you say you are now thinking about trying one day to write a new story about your time which you have been staying here with John and me. Now that will be the one book that I most definitely would like to read."

"Thank you, Mrs. Mary, for you have been more help to me these past few years than I could ever tell you. No Mrs. Mary, before you say anything, please let me finish my thoughts, as what I was going to say is that you have taken valuable time out of your day to read and correct mistakes in my writing. And it is not just this one: it has been all my writing since I've been here. If I do ever find the time to write about my time here with you both, I will see to it that you get one of the first signed copy. Who is to know—I might just find the time to work it into this story."

"Now, Clay, if you are wanting me to finish reading this for you, will you please go? You got tears forming in my eyes—wait, before you go, hand me my red pen from the end table."

"Yes, Mrs. Mary. I will get my pen and notebook and walk down to the beach and see if anything comes to mind that I can add to this story."

"Yes Clay, you do just that, and this time, see if you can give me more information to work with."

"Yes, Ma'am, I will do my best to see you when I return."

John is working down at motorcycle shop all alone and feels worried about how he's going to keep his business going, for there has been no sales in over three months. He is trying to think of ways he could get money coming in, and if that doesn't work, he may end up selling out.

He looks up at the clock. It shows half-past-three; he picks up the phone and calls his son Jorge, who owns the other motorcycle shop on the far west side of town, but he gets no answer.

Well, Mary and I will see them on Mother's Day; I will talk things over with them then. I am going to lock up and head on home, for it's been boring without Clay here for me to pick on. I wonder what he has been doing all day? Knowing him like I do, he's been out chasing women all day.

As John is now on his way home, he stops by to see one of his oldest friends, Zeke, who has been asking him to go fishing. John gets out of his old work truck and walks up to the door and knocks.

Zeke's wife Tammy answers the door. "Well, hello, John, come on in. Zeke is in the backyard; I will let him know you are here."

"Thank you, Tammy."

She turns and proceeds to sashay her way to the back sliding door, and she says, "Hey Zeke, you old sugar bear, John here to see you."

"Well Tammy, tell him to come on back; we can talk out here."

"Yes, my sugar bear." Tammy sashays her way back to the living room and tells John, "Zeke said for you to come on out to the backyard."

As John heads towards the backyard, Tammy asks, "Would like me to fix you a cool glass of my special lemonade?"

"Yes, ma'am, that would be nice. Thank you."

As Zeke and John are talking about going fishing tomorrow, Tammy brings out their lemonade.

Zeke says, "Tammy, you know I have been after this old goat here for a long time to go fishing with me. Well, guess what? He has finally agreed to go."

"That is this great news; when are you two going?" John speaks up. "Tomorrow morning."

Zeke says, "Tammy, you are also going, right?"

"I do not know if I can: I have a lot of work to do here."

John says, "Tammy, I will tell Mary that you are going, and that way we will all be going, so what do you say? Will you go?"

"John, if you can talk Mary in to going, I will go."

Zeke says, "Yes, now you are talking! Now, my fine, lovely baby, we are going fishing tomorrow."

"Stop saying things like that: you are embarrassing me."

"Well, Zeke, I will see you both in the morning."

When John finally gets home and walks in, Mary greets him with a kiss and asks, "How's your day been?"

"Mary, my day when well, thank you for asking. What about yours?"

"Now, my sweet John, it could have been great if you'd been here, but other than that, it was okay."

"Mary, I may or may not have good news to share with you."

"What is wrong now?"

"You know Zeke's been after me for a while to go fishing, right?"

"Yes, I know, and what's wrong with that?"

"Well, I stopped by his house on my way home, and we talked it over with Tammy. We decided to go in the morning, and we would love for you to join us."

"Now John, are you telling me that after all this time, you finally decided to take time off to go fishing? Why, yes, I am going!"

"Great, then I will call Zeke and let him know we will see them at six o'clock in the morning."

Once John gets off the phone with Zeke, Mary asks him if he would read what Clay had written earlier.

"Later. Right now, I am going to the storage shed to look for our fishing gear."

A half hour later, John has yet to return from the storage shed. Mary walks out to see what has taken place.

"John, what is taking you so long?"

John looks around at Mary, scratching his head, and says, "We need to have a garage sale."

"Oh, you think so?"

"Yes, just look at all this stuff pack in here. I cannot find our fishing gear anywhere in this stuff. I am guessing that since I'm unable to find the gear, I am going to buy new gear tomorrow morning, when we get our license."

"Let's go in the house and I will fix you supper."

"Well, okay, let's go. I am getting hungry."

On their way back to the house, Mary lays a big wet kiss on John. "John, I got a big favor to ask of you."

"Wow, it must be a big favor for you to kiss me like that."

"Yes, the favor is very important to me. You recall me asking you to read what Clay wrote today?"

"So, what you're telling me is that he's been sitting in his room, trying to write about something worth reading?"

"Yes, and I feel that he has done well."

"Now, Mary, how many times must I tell you: that boy is not right in the head?"

"John, I strongly feel if you would read this, you would be calling Big Joe asking him to read it as well."

"Wait, little miss, if you think I will call Big Joe and ask him to read something that Clay wrote, well, it is going to take way more than a wet kiss."

Mary looks at John with a sweet smile on her face. "Well, just how much more would it take to convince you?"

"Oh, you know, Mary."

"Oh, John, you're not right for thinking that way."

As I walk into the kitchen where they are talking, they up look at me and stop talking. "Oh, I am sorry, I did not mean to interrupt your conversation Mr. John."

"No, Clay, you did not interrupt us: we were only talking about Big Joe. I asked John if he had heard back from him today."

"Mary also told me that you have been working on another story today; would you mind telling me a little about it?"

"Yes, sir, I have. Would you like to read it, now that I have made all the corrections Mrs. Mary suggested?"

"Well now, Clay." Mary bumps John's leg with hers under the table.

"Sure, why not? I have nothing better to do than to read about one of your stories. But before I read it, will you tell me a little about it? You know, just in case I may miss something as I am reading it."

"Sir, do you recall one day last week when you said you were taking Mary to see a screenplay?"

"Yes, I do remember that, but what does that have to do with your story?"

"John, I started thinking that I would like to try writing my own screenplay."

"Now Clay, you still have not told me what it is about."

"Well, you old hardheaded goat, you did not let me finish."

"John, I do believe Clay's got you there."

"Only you would believe that, Mary."

"Now look, you two, can I please finish telling what the story is about?"

"Yes, please do."

"Thank you, Mrs. Mary. Now, John, the story is about my very first book. I wrote my own version of a screenplay for it, and to top it off, guess what else? I am going to even write a theme song."

John is sitting there, scratching his head, thinking to himself: *Now this I must see for myself, for I do not believe he has the capacity to fall from a moving truck, much less write a song.*

"Now, John, are you still willing read it?"

"Yes, Mary I am going to; and I do understand now why you are wanting me to ask Big Joe to have a look at it."

After two hours passed, Mr. John finally finished reading my work on what I'm calling a screenplay.

"Well, what do you think about Clay's work?"

"Mary, I cannot believe it: he sure did a genuinely good job with this. It's mind-boggling, the way he was able to combine it all together, have it to sound completely natural, and it's lifelike in lots of ways. Mary, to be honest, at times I could see someone's life being played out before my very eyes."

"John, would you want to know something else?"

"Yes, what would that be?"

"If I do recall, he also said he was going to try writing a theme song of it. Now, why are you shaking your head?"

"Mary, I understand why you had asked me to call Big Joe and see if he would look at this, but I do not believe Clay can write a song."

"John, you said the same thing about him writing this, and you've eaten those words."

"No, Mary, I did not. As I think back as to what he said, I believe you may have written this for him."

"Now, honey, I only fixed what I seen needed corrected; now give me a kiss."

"Oh, yes Ma'am, I will be happy to give you a kiss. As I think back, did I not see where he gave an answer about who was knocking at the door?"

"What are you talking about?"

"Mary, where he says someone was knocking on the door. I am thinking whoever may one day reads this would like to know who it was. I am going to see if he will tell me who was at the door."

"Well, you do that, but do not take all night; we need to get our sleep if we are going fishing with Zeke and Tammy."

John goes to Clay's room and knocks on the door.

Clay opens the door. "Oh it is just the old goat; what can I do for you?"

"Clay, I would just like to tell you, after reading your story, how enormously proud I am in your accomplishment of writing sure a beautiful story. Now with that said, I must ask you this: just who was knocking at the door?"

"Mr. John, I know it was extremely hard for you to say that, and I know it was, so thank you. About your question, I will only say for now that the answer will remain a mystery. I do gratefully thank you for taking the time to read it; now, is there anything else that you would like to know?"

"No, Clay, I guess not." John turns and walks out going back to his own bedroom, where Mary asks him what Clay told him.

"Mary, he said the answer will remain a mystery."

"John, your question itself is a mystery."

"Oh, no it is not! You cannot leave people hanging like that; it is a question they will one day like to know the answer to."

"Whatever, John, I do not see how it is important. Just forget it and go to sleep."

"Yes, my love. May I get another one of your sweet kisses?"

"No John, for you have not said that would call Big Joe and ask if he would mind looking at Clay's writing."

"Mary, if I do not forget when we get back from our fishing trip, I will call and ask him then."

Early Friday Morning

I'm awoken by a sound coming from down the hall. I get up to see as to what it could be.

It was Mr. John going to the restroom.

We say good morning and John asks why I am up so early.

"Well, Mr. John, I heard this great noise, so I got up to investigate it, but I found it to be only you."

"Well, then Clay, you can go on back to bed. Mary and I are going on a fishing trip with Zeke and his wife Tammy today. Oh, Clay, before you go back to bed, there is something I need for you to do for me today."

"Mr. John, just what could I do for you?" I'm thinking, *Now could just be the time I've been waiting for to get even with the old goat for all the mean things he has been saying to me.*

"Clay, I would like for you to look after the shop while Mary and I are gone on our fishing trip; can you manage that for me?"

"Yes, sir. I be more than happy to look after things at the shop for you."

"Now Clay, I am counting on you to see everything goes smoothly."

"Oh, John, now you and Mrs. Mary have fun catching fish and just leave that old shop to me."

"Thank you, Clay, I am hoping we have fun. It has been a long time since I have gone fishing with Zeke."

After John finishes what he was doing, he walks back into the kitchen, where Mary was packing their food for the trip, and asks if she's ready.

"Yes, John, I am ready."

As they head to meet Zeke and Tammy, John stops and buys new fishing gear and their licenses. They arrive at the dock, and as they are getting out of John's old run- down shop truck, Mary sees Zeke waving.

John and Mary head to the boat, carrying their gear. Once John and Mary are aboard the boat, they all say good morning to one other. Tammy and Mary start talking about how things have been since they last talked. Mary begins to tell Tammy that Clay has once again started writing toward what may become his fourth book one day.

"Now Mary, I know you did not just say that he has drafted another book. What could he have writing about this time around?"

"Now Tammy, from what I have read of it, it is about this endless dream, or maybe a screenplay about his first book. I am not sure: it seems to get a little fuzzy at times, but with the way he tied things together so well, it appears to me as if he took some lines from his first book. Even John could not believe how good it sounded after he had read it."

"Mary, has he said as to what the endless dreams are about?"

"Well, that is something I have been unable to get him to answer, because he says he's not completely done with it, and until then, he is not going to say anything."

"Mary, do you think he would mind if I read it and see what I can find?"

"I think he would love for someone else to read it other than John and me; I even told him I would try to

get John to convince Big Joe to have a look at it, and he was fine with that."

As the ladies are back in the cabin just talking away about Clay's so-called writing abilities, Zeke tells John, "Now this looks like a great spot to start fishing."

"Yes, Zeke, it does. Now, let me get my line in the water and find out if anything is biting."

Back at the house, I'm thinking about going by the coffee shop for breakfast before going on down to Mr. John's motorcycle shop. Before I go, I decides to take a nice hot shower.

As soon as I start to step into the shower, I hear someone knocking at the door. I grab my bath towel and wrap it around my waist before going to answer the door.

As I open the door, there stands the most beautiful blue-eyed young lady I've had the pleasure of ever laying my eyes on since the day Angela found me in that desolate desert.

She says, "Hello, are you Mr. John, by any chance?"

"Oh, Ma'am, I am sorry, I seem to have lost myself in your beauty for a second; well, you come on in and have a seat."

"Sir, do not you think that you need to get dressed first?"

"Ma'am, I was about to get into the shower when you came knocking."

"Oh, I am so sorry, sir, I hope that I did not come at an inconvenient time."

"No ma'am, come on in and I will get dressed and fix us a hot cup of coffee, and then we can start this conversation all over."

As I am getting dressed, she once again asks me, "Is your name Mr. John?"

"No, ma'am, my friends call me Clay."

"So, then you are not Mr. John."

"No ma'am, Mr. John and his wife Mary have gone on a fishing trip with their friends Zeke and Tammy."

"Well, Clay, do you know when they will be back?"

"Ma'am, here's your coffee, and no, they did not say just how long they would be gone, and I did not get your name."

"Clay, my friends call me Elizabeth, and I work for this company that Mr. John orders parts from. The owner has sent me here to find out why he has fallen behind on his monthly payment."

As she is telling me this, I start thinking, *Oh yes, baby my plans may have just starting to come together as to how I am going to get even with that John.*

"Now, Ms. Elizabeth, if you can just come back this Monday morning, I am sure you can get up with Mr. John and talk with him then."

"Thank you, Clay, and please tell him I will be back Monday morning to see him."

"Oh, no doubt ma'am; I will be sure to tell him you stopped by today."

Once she has left, I go take my shower and head to the coffee shop.

In the meantime, John and Mary are having the time of their life catching red snapper. John turns and says,

"Zeke, I have not had this much fun in a long time; man, we need to do this more often."

"Yes, John, we do at that."

Tammy speaks up. "Yes, we do. Mary and I said that very same thing no more than ten minutes ago. We were talking about asking you both about us coming back on Memorial Day weekend."

Zeke says, "Well John, what have you to say about us doing that for Memorial Day?"

"Oh, come on, John, just say yes, and we can ask Clay to join us."

"Now Tammy, I would love to come back out here on Memorial Day, but there is no way under the sun I am going to ask Clay to come."

"Now, why do say that?"

Mary says, "Tammy, Clay does not like to be in deep water; he had told us that he almost drowned and to this day he does not care about being out in a boat."

"Now Mary, be honest here: you know that is not my reason for not asking him to join us."

Tammy looks at Zeke. Zeke says to John, "I was under the impression that you like have Clay around."

"Zeke, I do at times, but he has this way of getting on my nerves. Just the other morning, he started trying to sing while in the shower."

"Just what is wrong with that? Zeke does it all time when he in shower," Tammy says. "If I were a betting man, which I am not, I would say he does not sound as bad as Clay."

Mary could not help but to laugh as John was saying that about Clay's singing in the shower.

John looks at Mary and says, "You know that was not funny."

"No, John it was not, but the way you jumped up from the table that morning shanking your head sure was."

Tammy says, "Well, John, just what was he singing about?"

"Oh, believe me Tammy, you do not want to know."

"Yes, I do."

"Okay, Tammy, just remember now you are the one who has asked me to sing."

As I am on my way, I find myself thinking why Mr. John has fallen behind on his payment. I walk into the coffee shop and see Kim standing behind the counter. I walk up to the counter and take a seat.

"Well, good morning, Ms. Kimm how are you today?

Is Mary Ann or Sue working today?"

She looks at me with those sassy little green eyes and says, "No they are not; they will be here after lunch. Would you like to leave them a message?"

"No, Ms. Kim, I will stop by after work and see them."

"Your other sweet lady has started working in the kitchen today; would you like for me to tell her you are here?"

"Oh, no, Kim, please do not tell her I am here."

"Well then Clay can I get you something to eat?"

"Yes, Kim, I would like two eggs sunny side down with a bowl of grits with butter, and my toast topped with strawberry jelly— wait now, Kim, that is not all—I would also like four pieces of bacon, slightly crispy, and two cool glasses of orange juice."

"What? No coffee to top off your order with, Clay? No ma'am, I already had a cup, but thanks for asking."

After eating, I am on my way to the shop. Once at the shop, there are two men waiting there, who ask where Mr. John Ndamukong is at this morning.

I now find myself, for the second time, being questioned about Mr. John Ndamukong's whereabouts. Being the smart guy I am, I answer them: "Now, if John Ndamukong wanted you to know his whereabouts, I am sure he would have called and told you; at least, I think he would have, anyway."

The two men reach inside their coat pockets and pull out their identification and show them to me. One says, "Now, are you going to tell us just where Mr. John is, or we going to take you downtown with us? It is your choice."

"Well, now excuse me, Mr. John has gone deep-sea fishing and I do not know when he be back, sir."

"Well, we need for you to tell John Ndamukong we're going to be here Monday morning at eight to talk with him.:

I'm thinking, *I am smelling my cake and it's almost done, and I cannot wait to put the icing on it tonight when I tell Mr. John.* "Oh, yes sir. I will be sure to tell him you two stopped by and that you will be back Monday."

Now, as I go about my daily routine here at the shop, around noon I began to wonder why these people came by to see Mr. John. I sure hope Mr. John has not gotten himself in any trouble. Now I know why Miss. Elizabeth said she had come by, but why did the two investigators come as well? That I do not understand.

Later that afternoon, Mr. John, Mary, Tammy, and Zeke have gotten back to the fishing dock after an enjoyable day of fishing.

Zeke turns and says John: "We can take the fish over to the fishing house and them clean and dress them there."

'Yes, Zeke that would be great, and while we are doing that, the ladies could be loading our gear up."

As Mary and Tammy take the gear back to the truck, Mary tells Tammy how far along she feels Clay has come with his writing ability.

While Zeke and John are having their fish cleaned, Mr. John begins telling Zeke he may have to close or sell shop.

Zeke asks, "Why would you do such a thing as that, John?"

"Zeke, it is like this: somehow, I have fallen behind on my payment, and I have not been able to sale not one motorcycle in the past three months."

"John, I hope you do not mind me asking this, but have you said anything to Mary or your two sons about this?"

"No, Zeke, I was thinking of just waiting until Mother's Day. That way, we all can be together, and hopefully they can give me suggestions about what I should do. You know, I am getting on up there in age."

"Well, I hope you get it figured out, John, for I would not want to see you lose everything you have worked for your whole life."

Back at the trucks, Tammy asks Mary if she could come over one afternoon and read Clay's writing.

"Tammy, you and Zeke could come over tonight for supper and you could read it then. That is, if he does not have it down at the shop, adding more to it."

"Mary that sounds great, but I will need to ask Zeke first to see what his plans are for tonight."

"That sounds great; if he says yes, then we will sit on the front porch, and just reminiscing about the old times as they cook the fish."

John and Zeke return to their trucks. Before Tammy has time to say anything to Zeke, Mary asks Zeke if he would like to come over tonight for a fish fry.

Zeke looks at Tammy. "Well yes, I'm good with us doing that if John does not mind having us over tonight."

John answers, "You know I do not mind. Mary can ride home with Tammy, and you and I can stop on the way and pick up all the fixings."

"Now John, be sure to pick up the peanut oil along with all the fixings for the baked beans, and you best not forget potato salad and coleslaw and the hushpuppies mix, because if you do, you know just where you will be sleeping for the next few months."

John nods. "Yes, my dear, will there be anything else?"

"Well, John, not that I can think of, but if I do, I'll just call you. Oh, wait, there is one more thing, John."

"Now just what would that be, Mary?"

"Now John, you know you will not use that tone of voice when talking to me: I am not Clay; now please, honey, will you get me a half-gallon of buttermilk for the hushpuppies mix?"

Mr. John thinks, *If I did not love that beautiful woman, like I do, I would still be on my own to this very day.*

Zeke and John are at the store getting all the things which Mary had asked them to pick up. As they walk up to the cash register, John reaches for his wallet, but Zeke stops him and says, "No John, I got this."

John says, "Thank you, Zeke."

As they head home, Zeke looks over and says, "John, you do not mind me asking you a personal question, do you?"

"Well, no Zeke, I do not mind you asking me a personal question."

"John, I want to ask: just how much money do you owe on your back payments?"

"Well Zeke, I believe it to be between thirteen to fifteen thousand dollars; now, that does not include the interest, which I do not have. Like I said earlier, I am three months behind, and as you well know, the interest rates are at an all-time high."

"Now John, we have been friends from the beginning of time, and I would like to extend my hand to you: if there's any way I can help you, I am here for you. Now as for me helping with Mrs. Mary, you are on your own."

"Zeke, why would you be saying that about Mary?"

"The way that woman spoke to you back at the dock this afternoon."

"Oh, is that what you are referring to? That's nothing: we talk like that to each other all the time. Now we need to get home and start cooking these fish, because if do not, you will hear some words coming from Mary—wait, what am I thinking? She doses love to make-up after a good argument."

As Mary and Tammy wait for Zeke and John to return, Mary tells Tammy she will go look in Clay's room to see if she could find the notebook which he has been writing in.

Tammy says, "Okay Mary, I need to use the restroom too."

"Tammy, the restroom is the second door on the right as you go down the hall."

"Okay, thanks Mary."

Now this afternoon, everyone seems to be doing their own thing. I am still down at the shop, doing my work like Mr. John had asked. I look at the clock and it shows half-past-four, so I start cleaning up the shop. As I get the last of the tools put away, I go over to where Mr. John keeps his book records.

As I look through them, I begin thinking back to the time when we all had to spend a great deal of time here beneath this old shop, waiting out the storm that came almost two years ago this upcoming month, as I recall. I reflect on how that one night changed my life forever.

I was unable to fall sleep that night from all the thundering and lightning that was going on, so I got up from out of my bed and came in here and fixed myself a cup of coffee and sat at counter over there drinking it, watching the lightning as it flashed across the night sky. The wind was blowing so hard by the time Mr. John had returned, it took both of us to open the shop door. There were all these people who were trying to come in; he up and left the door open for them and ran over to this very bookshelf, pulled one of these books downward, and the bookshelf began to open up.

Once it had fully opened, we started going down these stairs one by one into this place that appeared to me like a small city. Its hallways were like a small country with side roads going all over the place.

I stand here now, trying to shake off those memories of a time not so long ago, but it does not seem to be working. So, I am just going to lock up the shop for today and head out.

I am thinking of stopping by the coffee shop to see Mary Ann or Sue before heading to Mr. John's to tell him what has been taking place while he been off fishing.

As I walk, memories of another time begin to flash before me. When I first came here with the most beautiful woman, we were riding on the back of her camel. These memories take me back to which she first found me lying face-down in the desert sand; I remember her turning me over onto my back, and she touched my parched lips with drops of her cool water. I opened my eyes, and that is when I first laid my eyes upon Angela.

To this day, I have never met a more beautiful woman than her. If you saw her when she smiles, you would say her cheeks glow as bright as the sun shining on its brightest day. I remember that day when she took me back to her father's house to nurse me back to health, for she had me on her camel's back behind her. Her long, silky, autumn hair draped across her smooth, sexy, bare shoulder. I covered my face with her hair to block the sun, as it was beaming down on me, and her hair had a sweet smell to it: like coconut milk.

As I walk into the coffee shop, those memories of a time so long ago slowly fade back into their own little places.

Sue says, "Hello there, handsome, how's your day been?"

I stop and look around to see who she was talking to, for I did not believe she was telling me that I was handsome.

"Clay, are you looking for someone?"

"Yes, Sue, I was looking to see just who you were talking to; I just thought someone may have walked in behind me."

"No, Clay, I was only talking to you. Now, can I get you something?"

"Oh, yes Sue, I will have a steak with a baked sweet potato, and a glass of your sweet tea with a slice of lemon."

"Now Clay, how would you like your steak cooked?"

"Well, Sue, I am thinking I would like for it to be cooked on the grill."

Sue gives me that look that could kill and says, "Oh really now, Mr. Smarty-Pants? Now, really tell me how you would like your steak cooked."

"Let me see…"

When I said that, Sue just smiled and started shaking her head. "Oh here we go again."

"Sue, I would like it medium-well please. Will you ask the cook to season it with freshly cracked black pepper and kosher salt, and then add flaky sea salt, and some chopped herbs like thyme, rosemary, or sage to top it off?"

"Now, that's more like it. I will get your order going. In the meantime, drink your sweet tea and suck on your lemon."

As I am sitting here eating steak, in walks Gloria; she is wearing a low-cut pinkish tank top pulled down on her shoulders, with a short blue jean skirt only inches above her knees and these two-tone brown cowgirl's boots. I am captured by her beauty and can only watch as she sashays across the room, heading toward my table.

She says, "Hello Clay, I was not expecting to see you here this evening. Would you mind if I join you?"

"Oh, yes, Gloria please do. it nice to see you this evening; would you like for me to order you a steak?"

"Yes, Clay, I do believe I would like one, thank you." Mary Ann and Sue are standing behind the counter:

they see us sitting together and start talking.

Mary Ann says that if she was looking to hook up with Clay tonight, she may be heading for a big disappointment.

Sue says, "Mary Ann, I would not be so sure of that: you know her kind."

They see that I am waving for one of them to take my order, and they both just throw their heads back, turn, and walk into the kitchen.

"Well, Gloria, I do believe neither of them saw me waving after all."

"Yes, Clay, they saw you: I saw them looking over here.

They just do not like me."

Jenny comes over to our table and asks, "Is there something you need, Clay?"

"Yes, Jenny, could you please get my friend Gloria here a nice steak? Ms. Gloria how you would like your steak cooked?"

"I prefer my steak cooked medium, only three minutes on each side, and I'll have a glass of tea with a chef salad and thousand island dressing, please."

"Well Ms. Gloria, would you also like a baked loaded potato or a sweet potato?"

"No, thank you Jenny."

"Yes ma'am, then I will get your order in for you."

"Thanks, Jenny."

"You're welcome, Clay."

Jenny takes Gloria's order back to the kitchen, then brings out her tea. "Ma'am, your steak will be out shortly."

While we wait for Gloria's steak to arrive, she and I are just talking and laughing. Sue saw us doing so and turned back to the kitchen door, motioning for Mary Ann to come out.

Now this time, Mary Ann comes out to see just what Sue wanted. I take Gloria gently by the hand and gaze softly into her beautiful hazel, blue-green-flecked eyes. "Gloria, I hope what I am about to say to you, you will never hold against me."

"Oh, Clay, I could never hold anything against you, you should already know that, so what are you wanting to tell me."

"Gloria, you are looking very lovely in your pinkish tank-top, pulled down on your smooth shoulders. Gloria, why are you blushing? I've only told you what you already know."

"Clay, you are the only one who has ever said words like that to me before."

"Mary Ann brings Gloria's steak and salad and drops them with an attitude before asking, "Will you two be wanting anything else tonight?"

In disbelief with what Mary Ann had just done, Gloria and I just look up at her and I say, "No Mary Ann, but you sure can bring me the check. Thank you."

Once we had finished our meal, I pick up the check and we walk up to the counter to pay, and Mary Ann is standing behind the cash register. Gloria leans over and whispers in my ear, "Sweetie, I'll wait for you outside, big boy."

She walks out, I give Mary Ann a disgusted, angry look as I hand her only what I owe for the meals.

"Clay, why are you looking at me that way?" I shake my head and just walk out, leaving the answer for her to figure out for herself.

I meet Gloria outside and ask her if she would like to take that walk we had talked about taking on the beach before we go home.

"Oh, yes, I would love to take that walk tonight. It is a beautiful full moon shining bright tonight."

A Walk on the Beach with Gloria

As we are walking down to the beach, Gloria takes my arm, pulling me even closer to her.

I look at her with this big smile. "Gloria, you look even more beautiful out here in the moonlight, with the way the light reflects on you from the moon."

"Thank you, Clay. You are not looking so bad yourself, big boy."

"Well now, Gloria, what you are saying is I look better in the moonlight. Now why did you push me away?"

"Clay, you know just what I meant."

I put my arm around her sexy waist and pull her closer to me. "I know. I was only curious as to see what your reaction would be, but your response was not the one I was looking for."

"Well, I am sorry, Clay; what were you expecting me to say?"

"Well, I hope you'd say that I look handsome."

"Well Clay, what if I just do this instead of saying anything."

"Wow! I say you can do that as often as you like."

"So, Clay, you like my kiss better than me saying you look handsome in the moonlight."

"Gloria, before I answer, how about we just try that once more, just to be on the safe side?"

"Okay, just remember you asked for it, Clay."

"That was a double whammy! I saw stars for those eight seconds."

"Clay, would you like to try one of my triple whammies now?"

"I am afraid to ask you what a triple whammy is, but okay.

"Why am I on my knees and why's everything spinning around? Did something just hit me?"

"Clay, are you okay?"

"No Gloria, I feel very dizzy from everything spinning; I need to lay down here for a minute or two and see if the spinning will stop."

I reach out and pull her down closer to me, whispering, "Girl, you got a kisser on you unlike any other I've kissed before."

"Can we try once more?"

"Sure, why not? The spinning has stopped."

Ten minutes later, I whisper in her ear, "We got to stop before it become more than just kissing, Gloria."

"Oh, I see, but must we stop now, just when everything is going the way I was hoping it would?"

"Yes, Gloria that is the very reason we need to stop now, for I do not want to do anything that would disgrace you or myself in that way. I have more respect for you than that, and I do not care for one-night romances."

"Clay, who says this must be a one-night romance?"

"Gloria, you know I went through a very nasty divorce a few years ago. From going through that, I feel within my heart that I could not manage another intimate relationship with any other woman without me first getting to know more about her than what I once thought I knew about my first wife."

"Clay, I understand where you are coming from, for I feel the same way, but will you promise me something if I promise you the same?"

"Gloria, just what kind of promise are you wanting me to make you?"

"Clay it's a simple one: if I promise that I will not date anyone from this night forward, will you promise me the same?"

"Wow Gloria, I am not seeing that as a simple promise to make. I going to need time to think this over before I can make you a promise like that."

"Clay, will you let me know no later than, say, Mother's Day, if you can?"

"Sure, Gloria, I believe I can get you an answer by then; now, may I walk you home?"

We arrive at her house; she lays another wet kiss on me, then says, "Good night, handsome."

I say, "Good night, my sweet beauty, sweet dreams."

Back at Mr. John's house, Tammy and Mary are sitting on the front porch. Tammy turns to Mary and says, "From what I have read of Clay's writing so far, I am loving reading this, but I do not understand why he did not finish the story about Susanna being in the hospital; if he had finished it, I believe it could be a great story."

Mary says, "Look Tammy, there comes Clay walking up the sidewalk. Once he gets here, you can ask him why he did not finish writing about her being in the hospital."

As I make my way up the steps, Mrs. Mary says, "Clay, Mrs. Tammy has been reading your writing and has a question for you."

I say, "Hello Mrs. Tammy. So you have read my writing, therefore I have a question for you: what are your thoughts about it?"

"Clay, my thoughts are that if you had finished telling the story about Susanna being in the hospital, I believe it could be a lovely book for someone to read."

"Clay, you need to take a deep breath before answering her."

"Mrs. Tammy, as I was writing that prat of my story, there was a lot going on in my life that took up a great deal of my time, therefore I did not find the time to finish it, but since you brought it up, I will see if I can find time to finish it just for you. Now, Mrs. Tammy, is there anything else you would like to know?"

"No, Clay not that I can think of now, other than once you have finished writing it, I would like to read the rest of it, if you do not mind."

"Oh, no ma'am, I would not mind at all. In fact, I would love for you to read it. Now, Mrs. Mary, where is Mr. John?"

"Clay, he is around the back, talking with Mr. Zeke."

"Before you go, there's something I just remembered that I would like to say about your writing."

"Yes, Mrs. Tammy, what might that be?"

"Now, please, Clay, do not take this the wrong way, for I am only telling you this as a friend: I did find a few places where you could use vast improvement. For instance, in your plotting and pacing; throughout most of your story, you jump around a great deal. Now, take someone who has bought your book and started reading it for the first time: I feel they would find it too be hard to follow. Like here in the screenplay, you went from one scene of the screenplay to having Floyd and Jimi, who are writing another bizarre screenplay for Big Joe, making it impossible to follow where you were going with your story. I was having to guess what was happening during that time."

"Okay now, Mrs. Tammy, I do thank you for being very observant about the bizarre screenplay. I am going to try to explain this to you all that the screenplay which Big Joe has Floyd and Jimi working on is a screenplay that I had written about my very first book a few years earlier, 'As the Journey Begins.'"

"So, Clay, what you are telling me is that there has been a screenplay written about your very first book?"

"Yes, Mrs. Tammy, that is correct."

"Wow, Clay, that is great, for there are many great books out there that do not get a screenplay written about them unless someone has found it to be worthy. Will you be willing to tell me how this all came to be? If you do not mind, of course."

"No, Mrs. Tammy, I do not mind if we keep it between just us for now."

"Clay, I must say that keeping this just between us would not in any way help the person who is reading to understand the story."

"Hmm, well, Mrs. Tammy, let me try to answer you in a manner that will help without me giving away the entire story here. Now, in the beginning of my stories, which have been written about myself, I was referred to as Son, who has found himself to be on this quest in search of my new soulmate after having gone through a very ugly, nasty divorce some years earlier."

"Oh, Clay, I am so sorry. Mrs. Mary did not tell me that you have gone through a divorce."

"Well Tammy, I did not because I felt if Clay wanted you to know, he'll tell you."

"Wait, Mrs. Tammy and Mrs. Mary, let us not get into an argument over nothing. Now, after my divorce, I decided to try writing about a man beginning a journey looking for a Godly woman who has true biblical wisdom and fears our Lord, and in doing so, it has become an endless dream for the characters. Now, Mrs. Tammy, did I answer your question?"

"Well, yes, you did, but what I really would like to know is just where this dream takes your character to find his new soulmate."

"That Mrs. Tammy, I cannot say for sure just yet; but it appears to be a desolate, deserted place, where women just do not seem to have much interest in having a one-man and one-woman relationship anymore; it seems it has gotten to this point where you might say it's become a runaway wild jungle."

"Well, Clay, may I ask just what you mean by that statement?"

"Now, Mrs. Tammy, Mrs. Mary, I try to explain it like this: when you have men who are sleeping with other men and then there are also women who are sleeping with other women, and when there are those who are sleeping around on their own spouses and they all find nothing wrong in participating in such an ungodly act, well, if that does not sound like a wild jungle, then I do not know of anything else that you might could call it. But you both want to know something else? The saddest part of this all is that there are these churches that is teaching them that God sees nothing wrong with their behavior. Mrs. Tammy, Mrs. Mary, may I ask you both this question?"

Tammy gives me this crazy, bizarre look and looks over at Mrs. Mary.

Mary says, "Well, it all depends on what kind of question you are going to ask."

"Well okay then, let me try asking it this way: how can any true God-fearing church, who truly believes God's words to be true, say that God finds no wrong in people living that way, for I find in my bible that it says it is an abomination in God's eyes. Now, can either one of you tell me the answer?"

They both just pause with a puzzled look on their faces.

Mary says, "Now Clay, not all people believe that way. Take my daughter Lana: she is a true, God-fearing woman who holds true to her beliefs very strongly. That is the very reason why she has not gotten married."

"Mrs. Mary, are you saying that Lana believes that there is not a man in this world who is worthy of her love?"

"Oh! Now Clay, do not go putting words in my mouth that I did not say; what I meant was that she has not met the right man."

"Not to be sound rude, Mrs. Mary, but I got to talk to Mr. John. Did you say he's around back?"

"Yes, Clay, he is in the back."

"Thank you, and Mrs. Tammy, it was nice meeting you."

"Clay when you are done writing the rest of your story about Susanna, I would like to read it."

"Yes Mrs. Tammy, I'll ask Mrs. Mary to let you know when I have finished it, and Mrs. Mary, my plans for Mother's Day have changed: I will not be going with you over to Lana's."

"Now Clay, you know Lana is looking forward to seeing you."

"Yes, ma'am, I will give Lana a call later tonight and explain to her that something has come up that I must address, and I only hope that she will understand."

Now I go around back to tell Mr. John what took place. "Well, good, I have found you right where Mrs. Mary said you would be, Mr. John."

"Well, Clay, it nice to see you too; I was beginning to worry that something may have happened down at the shop."

"Oh, yes, Mr. John, something did happen at the shop, but first I need to tell you that a Ms. Elizbeth stopped by here this morning. She told me that she works for this company you order your parts from, and she continued

to say her boss sent her here to find out why you have stopped making your monthly payments."

"Okay, Clay, I understand her coming to find out why I'm falling behind on my payments, but Clay, I am more concerned about what happen down at my shop today."

"Now, Mr. John, I do not know why, and I did not ask, but when I got to your shop this morning there where these two law investigators with badges who said they were looking for you. I told them that you had taken the day off to go deep sea fishing with your friend Zeke. They then told me to tell you they would be back Monday morning at eight o'clock, and they were going to take you downtown with them for questioning."

"Say what! Clay?"

"Wait, Mr. John, sir. As I had said before, I am not sure what kind of questions they are needing to ask you, for I am only relaying the message they gave me."

As I am telling Mr. John this, I look over at Zeke and I can tell by the look on his face that he is thinking about something.

Zeke is thinking: *Just what I have gotten myself into here by telling John earlier that I would help him out?*

Now that he is being investigated, I just might need to back up and just reconsider my offer, because he never mentioned anything about this being a part of his problem.

Mr. John looks over at Zeke and shakes his head because he is unsure why he is being investigated.

Zeke asks John, "Just what have you done that these guys need to question you about?"

"Zeke, I have no clue as to why they want to question me."

"Now, Mr. Zeke, sir. It was nice meeting you, but I got other things I need to do, so good night to you both."

"Yes, Clay it was nice meeting you as well; now John, I have enjoyed our day fishing and the supper as well. It's gotten late, and Tammy and I need to be heading home, for I hear my bed calling me."

"Yes Zeke, I also enjoyed our time together, and I am looking forward to our next fishing trip. Now, you and Tammy have a safe trip home."

"Mary, thank you for having us over here for supper this evening; I will call you tomorrow."

"Okay Tammy, good night."

"Now John, why do you have that look on your face?"

"Mary, there is something I need to tell you about. Let us go inside and sit down."

"Now, John, what is this about?"

"Well Mary, I am not sure how to tell you this, but Clay told me that two men were at the shop this morning when he got there. They were looking for me and they were going to take me downtown for questioning."

"John, did Clay say why they were looking for you?"

"No, Mary, he only said what they told him to tell me, and that was they would be back Monday morning at eight."

"Well, John, do you know why they would need to question you?"

"No, Mary, I have not the first clue what they want to talk to me about. Now, Mary there is one more thing I was going to wait until Mother's Day to tell you and the two boys about, and that is I have falling three months behind on my parts payments."

"Now, John, how did that happen?"

"Mary, there has not been anyone buying motorcycles for the last four months, so there has not been any extra money in the shop bank account to pay what is owed on the parts."

"John, just how much do we owe on these parts?"

"Mary, I believe it to be somewhere between thirteen to fifteen thousand dollars; that does not include the interest."

"John why have you waited until now to say anything to me about this?"

"Mary, this is my problem, and I am the one needing to figure out a way to fix it; that is why I was just going to wait and talk with my two sons."

Mary sits back on the couch and puts her hand up to her chin, thinking what is happening here.

"Mary. what is going on in that brain of yours? I can tell when you are thinking about something."

"No, John, there is nothing for me to think about. I am going to bed and will let you just figure this out, since that's the way you feel about all of this. Now, good night."

Mary then stops by my room and asks just what the two men were wanting to see John for today.

"Mary, they only told me that they needed to ask him some questions. That's all they told me, other than that if I did not tell them where Mr. John was today, they would be taking me downtown for questioning, so, I told them that he had gone on a fishing trip with Zeke. They then told me to tell Mr. John that they would be back at eight o'clock Monday morning to see him."

"Okay, thank you, Clay, and good night."

"Same to you, Mrs. Mary."

Shortly after she left my room, here comes Mr. John interrupting me writing the rest of the story about Susanna.

Early Saturday Morning Sunrise

The clock shows 4:15 a.m. and I am lying in bed, unable to sleep, thinking about what Gloria had said to me about us making each other this promise to not date anyone else.

I get up and tiptoe my way to the restroom so I don't wake Mr. or Mrs. John. I take a hot shower. As I am standing under the warm shower, letting the water run down my face, I try not to think any more about Gloria's ultimatum, but I am unable to get it out of my mind.

Once I am done taking my shower, I dry off and get dressed, then brush my teeth and fix my hair for an awfully long day.

As I'm returning to my room, I hear someone opening Mr. John's bedroom door: it was Mrs. Mary. She asks me if there's anything wrong.

"No, Mrs. Mary, there is nothing wrong." I then ask her if she's going back to bed.

She says, "No, I am not. It is time for me to get Mr. John's breakfast started; he will be getting up shortly, asking me if I got his breakfast ready."

"Oh, okay Mrs. Mary. There is something that I would like to talk to you about, if you do not mind."

"Clay, you know I do not mind talking to you about whatever's on your mind."

"Okay then, Mrs. Mary, give me, say, five minutes to finish getting dressed, then I will come to the kitchen, and we can talk about what has been bothering me throughout the night."

"Clay just what has been bothering you?"

"Mrs. Mary, is all right for me to ask you if anyone ever gave you an ultimatum, say, for instance, someone who you felt may one day be the person that you fall in love with?"

"Now why are you asking me that kind of question?"

"Mrs. Mary, do you remember me telling you that my plans had changed?"

"Yes Clay, I remember you telling me that."

"Well, Mrs. Mary, that would be why I had to change them."

"Clay, what makes you feel as if this person gave you an ultimatum?"

"Mrs. Mary, at first, I did not give much thought to it being an ultimatum until it just kept gnawing at me as I was trying to sleep. I feel that the person who I care about has given me one, and I am not sure how to handle it, being that it's right after my divorce."

"Well now, Clay, I going to say it would all depend on what kind of ultimatum the person gave me, as well as how the person presented the ultimatum to me."

Mr. John walks in as Mary and I are talking, asking where his coffee is and taking a seat at the table.

"John, I will get your coffee in a minute: Clay and I are talking."

"Well, I am needing my coffee now, thank you Mary."

"Mrs. Mary, thank you for talking with me about this; can we continue our conversation later, if you are okay with us doing that?"

"Oh, of course Clay, you know I do not mind."

"Well, Mrs. Mary, Mr. John, I am going to my room to get my pen and notebook, then I am going to take a walk down the beach to meditate on our conversation as it stands for now."

Once I leave the kitchen, John turns to Mary, asking what Clay's problem this morning was.

"Now, John, I do not rightfully know if he wants you to know his problem; I am sure he would say something to you."

"What were you two talking about when I walked in here?"

"Now, John, you are asking way too many questions which I feel like I need not answer. If you are that concerned about him, you need to be asking him.'

"Well Mary excuse me, there is no need for you getting all cynical about me asking you about Clay this morning."

"Well John if you need to know so bad, you stop him before he goes out the front door."

As I walk out the front door, Mary Ann is coming up the steps and says, "Good morning, Clay. I am glad to see you are up. Can we talk for a few minutes, if you do not mind?"

I look at her with a disgruntled look and say, "Yes, Mary Ann, I guess we can have a seat; now, just what would you like for us to talk about?"

"First Clay can you please stop looking at me with that disgruntled look? I already feel bad enough as it is: that is why I have come by to apologize to you for my uncalled-for rude behavior last night."

"Thank you."

"No Clay, before you say anything else, please let me finish what I have come here to say to you."

"Okay Mary Ann, you have five minutes, then I am walking on down to the beach to work on my screenplay."

"That's fine Clay, I am good with you giving only five minutes of you time, for I can you are still mad."

"Mary Ann, you now only have three minutes."

"Clay, it was not until I saw you sitting at the table, holding Gloria's hand, that my feelings for you got the best of me. I know that's not an excuse, but you must know, it just hurt me more than I can ever put into words, seeing you sitting there with her."

As I am listening to those words flowing from her beautiful rosy lips, my jaw felt as if it had dropped to the floor.

"Clay, do you remember the night we first had dinner together with Mr. John and his wife, and you brought Sue and me back to the parking lot?"

"Oh, yes Mary Ann, for that is one night which I will never forget, for you came on to me like a young roaring lioness that night."

"Okay Clay, I must confess something."

"Now, wait, Mary Ann, before you go any further, would you like to take a walk with me down to the beach, and we will continue this conversation there? That is, if you do not have to work today."

"No Clay, I do not have to work today, and yes, I would love to spend some time together at the beach with you, handsome."

A Beautiful Day at the Beach with Mary Ann.

Mary Ann and I are at the beach, and she is finishing her confession.

"Clay, as I was about to say earlier: from that very night, I have felt very strongly within my heart that I was falling in love with you. With every hour that I was not with you, those feeling seem to grow stronger, and I guess it took me seeing you holding hands and laughing with Gloria that night to bring those feelings forward."

"Mary Ann, I am glad you have confessed your feelings to me, but why have you waited so long to tell me that you felt this way?"

"Well, do you recall telling me how you felt about me coming on to you the way I did that night?"

"Yes, ma'am, I do remember telling you that I could not commit such an act without first knowing in my own heart that I was truly sure that I was in love with the woman."

"Clay, when you said that to me, it showed me just what a true man you really are, and Clay, those words have been pulling my own heart to love you that much more, more than I ever loved any other man before I met you."

"Mary Ann, there is something I must tell you now. You have just put me in a very awkward position, and I am not sure how to handle it."

"Well, Clay, why not just try saying what is on your mind?"

"That's just it, Mary Ann: I cannot just up and say what is on my mind without me first putting a great deal of time and thought into it, for this is a situation which I am not accustomed to finding myself in."

"Clay, why do you feel that way? Was it something that I said?"

"No, Mary Ann, it was not anything you said, but you are more determined to get me to say what is on my mind."

"Yes, I am. Now out with it."

"Okay, let me try putting it this way: I find you to be a beautiful person who I feel within my heart would be a great wife for me one day, but Mary Ann, until I can get my own emotions figured out and understand what true love really feels like again…I hope you understand me. After the way my first wife ripped my heart in two, I am just not sure if I can ever truly love another woman in that way again without first getting to know way more about her than what I thought I knew about her."

"Clay, you may not believe me when I tell you that my first husband had done me the same way. In the beginning, he was the man which I had always dreamed of having in my life. I can see from that look in your eyes that there is something else on your mind. What is it?"

"Mary Ann, I was only thinking about the situation I am in with you and Gloria."

"Now why are you still saying you are in a situation with Gloria and me?"

"Well, after you told me that you truly feel in your own heart that you love me, I can honestly say for the first time in my life I have had two women to tell me they were in love with me at the same time."

"What did you just say?"

"Mary Ann," I say.

"Stop right there; I know what you had said, but it took a second to register. Now Clay, just when did she tell you that she loved you?"

"Mary Ann, can we just go back to where you were telling me about your husband?"

"Yes, but not until you tell me more about Gloria."

"Man, I knew I should not have said anything."

"What did you just say?"

"Oh, nothing, I was only trying to think as to how I was going to explain the situation to you about Gloria and me being down here on the beach that same night you did what you did at our table. Now Mary Ann, please understand me, at the time this all took place, I did not know you felt that you were in love with me. Now after we left the coffee shop that afternoon, we walked down here and we started kissing, and she get me an ultimatum: if I promised her that I would not date other women and she would make me a promise not to date any other men."

"Well Clay, just what do you plan to do about this so- called ultimatum that she gave you?"

"Well, Mary Ann, I will promise you this: after I have a talk with her, you're going to be the only woman I will be dating from here on out. Now can we get back to talking about your first husband?"

"Clay like I was saying earlier, he was the man of my dreams, for he had asked me to marry him in my first year of college. But during that time, neither he nor I had a well-paying job to help finance me being in college."

"Wait Mary Ann, I do not mean to interrupt you, but what were you studying in college, if you do not mind me asking?"

"Well, Clay, I was going for my master's degree in human behavioral health. Now Clay, he and I only dated until I had finally gotten my master's degree, and then we got married and stayed together until he had gotten caught one day down at the boat ramp with another woman by one of my family members. Now Clay, can you believe this man had the audacity to stand before the judge and say that she was one of his co-workers, and the only reason that they were there was because they were working on some experiment?"

"As you well know, when a person does get caught doing something they're not supposed to be doing, they will try to use any excuse that they can produce to get themselves out of trouble."

"Well now, Clay, I am so glad you have said that."

"Uh-oh, did I just say something that I should not have said?"

"No, Clay you did not say anything wrong. I would just like for you to remember those words you said whenever you are having a talk with Gloria about the ultimatum."

"Mary Ann, why is that?"

"Because I would not like to be used as an excuse for you to not date other women. What I have told you is the truth and I meant ever last word of it, so please Clay, I am asking you to just be honest with her when you both talk. I admitted my love for you because I do not want to see you get hurt again."

"Mary Ann, I am going to be straight-up honest with you: I will do everything within my own limited power with the help of my God to not bring any kind of disgraceful shame upon you in anyway."

"Clay, I do believe you will keep your word just from judging your actions."

"Mary Ann, I also must confess to you: the night you did what you did in the parking lot of the coffee shop, I too felt you were the one I had been waiting for, but not knowing for sure what true love really felt like anymore, I could not tell you that I was feeling that way until now."

"Well Clay, I am glad that we both have now opened our hearts up and admitted the way we feel toward together, but there is just this one little thing which we have not talked about yet."

"Hmm, Mary Ann, I am afraid to ask what that one little thing is. Now wait, why are you looking at me like that?"

"Clay, I am only thinking why you have not told me about your first wife; have I not told you about my first husband."

"Mary Ann, I must tell you that I am not very strong when it comes to talking about that subject, so please, can we just sit here and enjoy our time together without bring up my wasted time with someone like her?"

"Clay, I can tell just by the sound of your voice that it hurts you more than anyone could ever imagine, but Clay, I can tell you, I have learned from my own past experience of going through a divorce. If you're not willing to talk about your feelings, you may never get over the hurt, and I do not want to see you become that person."

"Mary Ann, I will try telling you as much as I can, but if I become choked up on my words and just stop talking, just let me be okay."

"Clay, I promise if it is getting harder for you to talk, I will stop you, so why do not you start by telling me what you feel went wrong in the marriage?"

"Hmm, well now as I do think back on that, I am not so sure what went wrong, but this I can tell you: it seemed like every day, she just kept coming home later and later from work, so me being me, I just up and asked, 'Why are you coming home so late?" She spoke up and gave me this lame-brain excuse that she had these errands that she needed to take care of. Those so- called important errands that she needed to take care of was the needs of another man that she has been seeing behind my back, and I felt then it was time for me to let her go, for I could no longer see myself living my life with someone who just up and betrays the most sacred vows that one person could give another person."

"Clay, see, that was not particularly difficult for you to open up and talk about your failed marriage."

"I guess not, but that does not even begin to scratch the surface; now, would you like for me to continue?"

"Clay, yes, I would love for you to, but if you feel the need to stop with just telling me only this much for now, I understand."

"Okay, Mary Ann, we will change the subject and talk about just you and me, baby, for the rest of the day."

"Now Clay, that sounds sweet; are you trying to serenade me out here on the beach?"

"With a voice like I got, I cannot carry a tune to save my life, much less try to serenade a beautiful lady like yourself."

"Clay, I think you have a nice voice, if you had someone who could teach you how to sing, I believe that you would sound very lovely."

"Now that you have mention it, I've been thinking about trying to write a song. Would you have any idea how to start one?"

"Clay, why would you want to write a song? Well, Mary Ann, I had this screenplay written for my first book, and I would love to have a theme song for it, so I have been thinking about a song that would maybe describe the book."

"Well in that case, can you describe to me what the book is about in your own words? I will try to help you come up with something."

"Mary Ann, it is a story about this man who one day found himself on this journey looking for his new soulmate, and the journey takes him into desolate desert, but at times during his search for his soulmate, he finds himself having these bizarre flashbacks to when he was a young man married to this young lady."

"Oh, okay Clay, that should be easy. I am thinking we such start it off like this. 'I find myself once again searching for a true love unlike my first love, who had no knowledge of the meaning of true love. I am searching for someone who has the knowledge of knowing what true love really means: to love someone and not someone who's looking only to have just a one-night love affair.'"

"Wait! Mary Ann, I am sorry, but I do not feel that is what I had in mind as a theme song."

"Now Clay, you did not let me finish: I was just getting started."

"Mary Ann, I know, and I do thank you, but what I have in mind is something like this: 'I found myself awake from this dream; I was sitting on a cliff overlooking this old, rugged road we as young innocent lovers once traveled down. All I see today as I look out across this lonely valley is a cloud of smoke rising from the old wooden bridge that once joined our two worlds together as young lovers so long ago. As I now continue searching for my new love, as I sit here with only my tears rolling down my cheeks, I see in a small figment of rising smoke a face which reminded me of our journey we once begun so long ago. The tears that once flowed for a lost love flows no longer under that wooden bridge that once joined our two worlds together so long ago.' Now Mary Ann, that is more like what I have in mind."

"Oh, I see Clay, but I did not hear anything about where he is in the desert, looking for his new love-to- be."

"Yes, Mary Ann you are right. I have not come up with that part—that is where I was hoping you could help me out."

"Hmm, Clay, let me think on it for a little while and just see what I can come up with."

"Okay, my love, just take your time, for I am not in a rush."

"Mary Ann, there is one more thing I would like to ask you."

"Sure, Clay what would that be?"

"Mary Ann, do not take is the wrong way, but I would like to know what your biblical beliefs are."

"Clay, why are you asking me about my beliefs in God?"

"Mary Ann, I know that I said earlier that I felt as I was falling in love with you, but before I can ever make a commitment, I feel that I first need to know about the woman's commitment to her God."

"Well Clay, my commitment to God is a true one. Now if you do not mind, I would like for us to continue this conversation over dinner tonight, if you would like."

"Yes, Mary Ann, I would love for us to continue this over dinner, but first I need to have that talk with Gloria, then I will see you, okay?"

"That sounds great but remember what I had said about being honest."

Back at Mr. John's, Mr. John is having a conversation with Mrs. Mary about what has come up about the shop.

"Mary, I have been doing so thinking for some time now about just selling the shop and taking you away from here."

"Wait now, John, am I hearing you right? You want to sell your motorcycle shop and move away from here?"

"Yes, Mary that is what I said. You know I have always wanted to travel and see this world before I die, and you know we are not getting any younger."

"John can you please tell me where we would get that kind of money after you have said you are three mouths behind on your parts payment?"

"Mary, I am thinking that once we sell the shop and take out my 401k, I believe we would have enough to travel on, providing we watch how we spend our money."

"John, if this is your heart's desires, I'm fine with us doing this, but just when are you thinking about starting the process of selling the shop?"

"Mary, since you do agree, I will start this coming Monday after Mother's Day. That will give me time to talk it over with our children about us wanting to do this."

"John, do you think we need to wait and find out Monday what this investigation is all about first?"

"Now Mary, I believe there is nothing to worry about with this investigation, for I know in my heart I have done nothing wrong. Now, I am going to give Zeke a call and let him know that I am looking to sell the motorcycle shop."

"John, why would you be calling Zeke?"

"Mary, when I told him yesterday, I was behind on the parts payments, he said if I needed his help in any way, he would be happy to help, so I am asking for his help."

"Hello, Mrs. Tammy, this is John: may I speak Zeke please?"

"Sure John, give me a minute to get him. Hey, sugar plum, Mr. John would like to speak with you."

"Hey, John what is up, my friend?"

"Zeke, I am calling you because Mary and me has been doing some thinking about selling the motorcycle shop, and I was wondering if you may be interested in buying it."

"Well, just how much are you asking for the shop?"

"Well now Zeke, I know this may sound very high to you, but I am asking only one hundred and eighty-five thousand for the shop."

The phone went silent for a moment. "Zeke, are you still there?"

"Yes, John, I'm still here. I was thinking, to be honest with you, that I am not sure if I know of anyone who is willing to pay one hundred and eighty-five thousand dollars."

"Well Zeke, you know what I have invested in the shop, and I am willing to let everything that is there stay."

"Well, John, have you and Mary talked this over with the family?"

"No, Zeke, this is just from me and Mary. We're thinking we are going to tell them on Mother's Day."

"Okay, John let me know what they say about this, and in the meantime, I will check around and see if I can help find someone who may be willing to take it off your hands."

"Okay Zeke, I will talk to you on Monday. Goodbye."

"Sounds great, John. Goodbye."

"Zeke, what was that about?"

"Tammy, John is wanting to sell his motorcycle shop. He said that they are wanting to do some traveling which sounds like a great idea; maybe you and I need to start doing more traveling."

"Well, did he say when they would be starting their traveling around the world?"

"No, Tammy, that he did not say. He only said once he sold the shop for one hundred and eighty-five thousand dollars that they would start."

"Wait, Zeke, did I understand you? He is asking for one hundred and eighty-five thousand dollars?"

"Yes, that's how much he said."

"Zeke, sell my goat."

"Tammy, just what goat are you talking about?"

"You know, the one my great uncle James gave us for our wedding present."

"Have you forgotten that goat died two weeks after he gave it to us?"

"No, I am not talking about the one your uncle Jack gave us; I know that goat died."

"Well excuse me, I am sorry, I did not know that my uncle Jack gave us a goat as well, Tammy."

"Zeke, sugar plum, do not go getting an attitude with me."

"I was not getting an attitude."

"Stop that, Zeke, for I know what you said, and I was talking about my golden goat. It could not have died because it's been locked up in the vault down at the bank."

"Tammy, I had forgotten about you having that golden goat in the bank: he must be worth four times more than what John is asking for his shop."

Back to Mr. John's.

"Now, John what did Zeke say about you wanting to sell your shop?"

"Mary, he said that he would ask around and see if he could find someone who might be willing to buy the shop, but as for now, he do not know of anyone."

"Well, John, while you were talking with Zeke, I was thinking: what if you divide the inventory between the other two shops, then sell or maybe rent your shop? Do you think that would be an idea with which could work?"

"Mary, that is the best idea I have heard you come with in a long time; why did I not think of that before?'

"Because you are one hardheaded old goat like Clay says."

"Well now Mary there was no call for that. Why are you getting all cynical when I just gave you a nice compliment for coming up with a great idea?"

"Well now, it was all in the way the compliment came out of your mouth; it was as if you were saying I cannot think as good as you."

"Mary, I am going down to the shop to start the inventory would you like to come with me?"

"John, I cannot go with you because I got to get your supper done. Now just what do you want me to fix?"

"How about fixing fried chicken and mashed potatoes and brown gravy, and if you do not mind, your homemade peach cobbler, and I will pick up the vanilla ice cream on my way home."

"Yes, my love, I will do my best. Now if you by any chance see Clay on your way, tell him that Gloria has been calling for him."

"Yes, dear, if I see him, I'll let him know she is looking for him."

Now after I had walked Mary Ann home from the beach, I am on my way to have a talk with Gloria about the ultimatum which she gave me two days ago.

As I am walking by Mr. John's shop, I see him inside doing something, so I stop in to see what he is doing.

"Hello, Mr. John, what are you doing down here on Saturday?"

"Clay, that it is not any of your business, but Mary and I are going to sell out and do some traveling. Before I forget, Mary said to tell you someone by the name of Gloria has been calling, asking for you."

"Yes, sir I was on my way to see her when I saw you in here working, so I will be on my way. Thank you."

"Oh, Clay there is one more thing: Mary is cooking fried chicken and some mash potatoes with brown gravy, and for dessert, homemade peach cobbler."

"Mr. John, that does sound great, but I have told Mary Ann I would have supper with her, so I will see you both whenever I get back tonight."

Now after leaving Mr. John's shop. I head over to speak with Gloria. I find myself stopping at the park to do some thinking about how I am going to approach this situation which I have now found myself in with her and Mary Ann.

As I am sitting here on the park bench, watching the squirrels playing and the birds sing their love songs, I find myself thinking about this poem. It is a poem of a mother's love for her child.

"A mother's lovely beauty will outshine all other beauty when she holds the love of her child within her tender heart. Her love is an endless one, one which cannot be torn away from within her tender heart for her child, for the shine upon her face will forever shine as she awaits the arrival of her most precious innocent child. Her true innocent love for her child will one day take her on a path unlike any other she had ever travel before. A beautiful path of happiness unlike any she had ever known before, a path of sorrow to which she has never endured in her life, for only her innocent love for her child, who she knows was given to her by God. Now will this be what will see her though all the suffering of the pain in which she must endure in all of the days which lay before her innocent child? As she watches him growing up before her own eyes to become the man which she hopes for. For the sorrow she has felt from within her dreams have only shown her along the way that there is no hope for him ever becoming the man which God sent him here to be. For she now knows the dreams which she has had are all wrong: she knows without a doubt in her tender heart that God has put into place this plan for her innocent child's life which no sorrowing dream can change. For now, she can only hold to her belief in her God. She has once seen the worst of the sorrow which has been placed before her innocent child. She must now begin to bear her own life journey to understand this sorrowing pain which awaits her innocent child. There will come a day where no number of tears can drown the sorrow of seeing her lovely child nailed to an ole rugged cross, for such a sin has been placed up on her innocent sweet child's shoulders. She must once again suffer a much greater pain that no mother should ever endure in life, yet still she must forevermore let her innocent love outshine among all others, as she now makes that one last great journey to see her innocent child's face once again. For there can be no greater sorrow in one's heart than to see one of their loved ones leave this life without them first accepting the forgiveness of her innocent child love, our Lord Jesus Christ."

May the blessing of God be with you all, and thanks for letting this little book become a part of your book family. It is my hope you founded it to be somewhat enjoyable.

These stories which I have shared with you in this book are only just a figment of my own imagination. I hope you have enjoyed reading them as much as I have enjoyed writing them.

V/R Thank You.

George Mills